SEAL'S SKY (SPECIAL FORCES: OPERATION ALPHA)

BLACK EAGLE 4

LYNNE ST. JAMES

Dear Readers,

Welcome to the Special Forces: Operation Alpha Fan-Fiction world!

If you are new to this amazing world, in a nutshell the author wrote a story using one or more of my characters in it. Sometimes that character has a major role in the story, and other times they are only mentioned briefly. This is perfectly legal and allowable because they are going through Aces Press to publish the story.

This book is entirely the work of the author who wrote it. While I might have assisted with brainstorming and other ideas about which of my characters to use, I didn't have any part in the process or writing or editing the story.

I'm proud and excited that so many authors loved my characters enough that they wanted to write them into their own story. Thank you for supporting them, and me!

READ ON!
Xoxo
Susan Stoker

For Puppy, your star will shine bright in our hearts forever.
As always, for T.S., my real life hero. I love you!

ACKNOWLEDGMENTS

Thank you, Jessica, I couldn't have done this one without you, and this book is better because of it.

Special thanks to Lily who was there when I needed it most.

As always, my readers' group, the Coffee Crew, for always having my six.

I also want to thank the Melbourne Police Department, the Brevard County Sheriff's Department, and MJ Whitten at Thairapy Time, hairdresser extraordinaire – even if she'd prefer not to color anyone Sky Blue Pink.

NOTE TO READERS

I love Susan Stoker's books and being able to include them in some of my stories is so much fun. As with all my books, my use of her characters may not match with her books, but I do my best to keep them true to her series.

In **SEAL's Sky**, once again John "Tex" Keegan makes an appearance to help dig up information on a very nasty dude.

I hope you enjoy this story. If you do, I'd love it if you could leave a review. It's the best way to help an author.

Lynne
xoxo

CHAPTER 1

"Another fucking dead end. How the hell does he stay ahead of us?" Drew "Murph" Murphy sighed in exasperation. His impatience echoed that of the rest of the team. Four leads, four missions and they still hadn't captured Azfaar, the slippery son of a bitch.

The ex-Taliban terrorist managed to evade capture for almost a year since he'd initiated the kidnapping of a Missionary Group in Afghanistan. During the rescue mission, the SEALs neutralized Azfaar's brother and he'd vowed to avenge his death.

Ousted from his Taliban group by the leader of the province, he joined ISIS to continue his Jihad and carry out his threat against them. He'd made good on his promise with an attempt on their lives on American soil. It was too damn close for comfort and they wouldn't rest until Azfaar was either captured or dead.

'We'll get him," Jake Warner replied. He was the boss of the Black Eagle Team and just as frustrated as the rest of them. But losing their shit wasn't going to help.

"We'd better. Miranda still has nightmares at least once a week that he'll take her again," Cameron "Cam" Peterson added. Miranda, his girlfriend and the daughter of a US Senator was part of the missionary group that had been taken hostage.

It was their first run-in with Azfaar, and it hadn't ended well for him. The SEALs' mission to rescue the senator's daughter grew to include saving the rest of the kidnapped missionary group who were being held captive in a separate location.

Rescuing all of the hostages was a big win, but danger had followed them home. Homeland Security dropped the ball somewhere and some of Azfaar's men made it into the U.S.

It wasn't until months later that they realized the team and their women were being targeted.

Several attempts on their lives culminating with Miranda being kidnapped a second time and Cam and his K-9 Halo getting shot.

If it hadn't been for John "Tex" Keegan's help, they never would have found her in time. It wasn't the last time they'd be indebted to the medically retired SEAL with mad computer skills. When all else failed, he was their secret weapon.

"I hear you, Cam. When I walk in the door, Meghan gives me *that* look. Even though I don't say anything, she can read it on my face. The fear in her eyes is like a punch in the gut," Rafe Buchanan, second in command, said as he stowed his pack for the fourteen-hour flight home.

"Chrissy is doing all she can. Will you cut her some slack? It's not like Tex has done any better," Ryan McLaughlin, the team medic, said with an irritated sigh. Chrissy Stillwell, a former FBI analyst who helped identify and take out a massive terror cell, was his girlfriend. After the two of them took out the threat and shut down the cell, the CIA recruited her. Normally, she shouldn't have been involved in this case, but her best friend was Meghan, Rafe's woman. She and

Tex were working together to track down Azfaar's current location.

"No one's blaming Chrissy or anyone else. Chill your ass. Y'all will be buttering your biscuits soon enough," Murph said with his ever-present sarcasm.

The team changed a lot over the last year. It wasn't only the threat by Azfaar, it was the women who were now part of their 'family'. Of the five members of the Black Eagles, three were now in committed relationships. Only Jake and Murph were still single. Murph was by choice, but he had a feeling their boss was getting a little bam-bam in the ham on long weekends when he disappeared.

They were all getting soft, touchy-feely. It was ridiculous. They were freakin' Navy SEALs. He couldn't remember the last time they'd hung out at the range blowing off steam and going through a case of beers. Their after-action meetup at the Ready Room even included the women now.

"I know you're pissed off, but you all need to chill the fuck out," Jake said making a point to make eye contact with Murph. "We'll get him. No one is that good. He'll make a mistake and we'll be there. It's no different than the hundreds of other missions."

The team's nerves were raw and Murph knew better than to push their buttons. But he couldn't help himself, it was part of his nature and they knew it. It's not like he was jealous. No fuckin' way. The last thing he needed was a clingy woman waiting for him with a lot of questions he couldn't answer about where he'd been and then handing him a "honey-do" list. Even if a warm body in his bed and a little four-legged foxtrot would help him blow off some steam, it couldn't beat his personal freedom and the cozy apartment waiting for him.

Patting Halo, their German shepherd K-9, on the head, he headed for the cooler they kept stashed on the transport. Murph needed a beer but he'd have to settle for the root beer variety until he got home. A few cold brews would ease some of the tension still coursing through his veins. How the dirtbag asshat managed to stay one step ahead of them, he had no idea but it fucking sucked.

"What the hell is going on with you?" Jake asked as he came up behind Murph.

"Nothing. I'm good."

"Bullshit. Are you going to tell me you weren't trying to start something?" Sparks flashed in Jake's steel-grey eyes.

"No, maybe. I don't know. I'm sorry. I'm just…"

"I don't give a shit. You think it's all fun and games but dammit, you need to learn when enough is enough."

"Sorry, Boss. I'll work on it."

Jake searched his face for something and must have found what he was looking for. With a lift of his chin, he grabbed a soda and headed back to his seat.

Murph sighed. He didn't think he'd been that bad, but Jake didn't get pissed off for no reason. Unless there was something else going on they didn't know about yet. He really needed to get laid. It had been months since he'd had sex, and not because of lack of opportunity, more like lack of desire. It made no sense. He was the biggest horndog on their team. It was time he went back to his usual ways.

For the first time since he'd joined the Black Eagles, Murph felt alone, not lonely, more like isolated. It was his own fault. He'd gone out of his way to put distance between himself and the guys over the past couple of months. What he didn't understand was why he'd done it.

Seventeen hours later when their transport plane touched down at Naval Station Norfolk, Murph was no closer to figuring out his shit than when they took off from Bagram Airbase. Grabbing his gear, he followed the rest of the team off the plane.

"Debriefing at sixteen hundred," Jake reminded them as they walked across the tarmac. Not that any of them needed to be reminded.

"And we'll hit the Ready Room afterward?" Murph verified. Going home to his empty apartment after spending the last two weeks chasing down Azfaar was the last thing he wanted to do. It had become a tradition to go to their favorite bar to unwind after each mission. Meghan, Chrissy, and Miranda had been coming too. Truth be told, he enjoyed their company and he'd been worried at first that it would change the team dynamics, but they'd fit right in.

"Of course. You're an asshole, but we still love you, bro," Rafe answered for all of them.

"Glad to hear it," he said with his perpetual smirk. Happy he hadn't pushed them too far. As they crossed the airstrip, he inhaled the distinct scent of the ocean overlaying the stench of jet fuel and hot tarmac. It was just what he needed to shake off the darkness that hung over his head since they'd left on the mission.

Post briefing and fresh from the shower, Murph was the first to arrive at the bar. He and Ryan used to compete about getting first, but since Chrissy came on the scene, the old game was no longer a priority.

The bet he'd made last year was a sure thing for him. No way would he be serving drinks to the Team in a pink tutu. So why was he being such a jackass? On some level, maybe he did wish for what they had. But finding women who were as special as Miranda, Meghan, and Chrissy wasn't easy. Most of the females he met were after one thing—nailing a SEAL.

Pam smiled when he came in.

"Hey Pam, how are things?"

"Great. Everyone get back okay?"

They'd been hanging out at the Ready Room since they'd been stationed in Norfolk and Pam had always been there and knew all of the teams.

"Yup. They'll be here any minute now."

"The usual?"

Murph couldn't help but smile. He was always impressed by how she could keep track of what each team ordered. "Please."

Grabbing their table at the back of the bar, he pulled over the extra chairs they'd need. From his seat, he could see the front door and the doorway that led to the kitchen, restrooms, and rear exit. Murph surveilled the space and wondered what bug had crawled up his ass. Settling down was never his thing, he'd known that for as long as he'd been dating. Growing up with his parents' constant arguing had soured him on relationships. Seeing Rafe settle down with Meghan, and then Cam and Ryan finding love, made him dig in his heels.

As he waited for Pam to bring the beer, he watched her working behind the bar. She'd seemed fine when he came in, but now that she was on the phone she looked upset or worried, he couldn't tell from the table. It piqued Murphy's interest even though he knew it was none of his business. But being nosy was part of his DNA and he'd known her for almost ten years but didn't *actually* know anything about her.

Unable to restrain himself, he walked up to the jukebox and looked for a song. From there he could hear some of what she was saying, enough to know she was worried about someone. Upset enough that the color drained from her face. Not knowing what to do, he selected a song.

"Sorry about the wait."

"No worries. It gave me time to put on some music," he answered with a smile, hoping to make her smile in return. "Are you okay?"

"Of course. I'll be right back with some pretzels. Do you want me to get anything else?" The wobble in her voice belied her words.

Murph debated about asking her what was wrong but didn't think she'd appreciate him prying. So he resorted to his usual snark. "Not sure, we'll have to wait until everyone gets here. I'm sure they'll have worked up their appetites after riding the bony express."

"Oh my God, Murph." Pam burst out laughing. "Do you ever run out of those?"

"I haven't yet," Murph replied with a big smile. He was happy he'd been able to distract her for at least a moment or two.

"I hope I'm still here when you do."

"I dunno if you really want to do that. I have a very long list."

"Why am I not surprised? I bet you look for every chance to use them too," Pam said, shaking her head.

"I can neither confirm nor deny that statement."

This time Pam's smile reached her eyes and she looked more like herself. "You're a good man, Murph. I wish…"

He wasn't sure if she'd have finished what she was going to say or not, but they were interrupted when the rest of the Black Eagle Team filed through the front door. As usual, Halo accompanied Cam and Miranda. It was another thing they appreciated about the Ready Room, no one objected to the K-9s hanging out with the teams.

"Hey Pam, how's it going?" The guys asked as they saw her.

"Great, thanks. I'll be right back to check on you and bring Halo's water."

"Thanks," Cam answered as he and Miranda sat down. Halo took his usual position between their chairs.

The others grabbed seats until the table was almost full. Only their captain, Tony Knox, and Jake were missing.

"Is Jake coming?" he asked.

"Not sure, he said something about a call he had to make. But he said he'd try," Rafe answered as he filled two mugs at a time and passed them around the table.

When everyone's glass was full he raised his for a toast. "All in, all the time." The rest of the guys repeated the words and took a drink.

It made Murph think about Pam once again. He couldn't shake the feeling that she was in trouble. "Be right back," he said as he got up from the table. Rafe nodded in acknowledgment. If it ended up they could do something to help Pam he'd fill them in, but until then there was nothing to tell.

As he tried to come up with a good reason for butting into her business, she came out of the kitchen with water for Halo.

"Hey, I can take that for you," Murph said as he reached to take the bowl.

"You don't have to." When she met his eyes, they were red-rimmed and puffy.

That sealed it. "I know I don't. Feel free to tell

me to fuck off, but it looks like you got some upsetting information and it's obvious you've been crying."

"I'm fine, really."

"If you're sure, but if you need anything, let me know. Anything at all. You've been part of my life for a long time and seen us through some bad shit. I want to help if I can."

'Thank you, I appreciate it, really. But I'm fine.'

He didn't believe her, but unless she talked to him about it, his hands were tied. "Okay, just remember the offer is always open."

"Well, since you did offer to help, do you want to bring Halo his water and I'll grab the pretzels?" Pam asked holding out Halo's water.

"You got it." The niggling worry in his head wouldn't go away, maybe he would talk to the guys about it. Because until she came to them for help, he couldn't think of anything else to do.

CHAPTER 2

"Hello?" The suspicion in Pam Turner's voice came across loud and clear.

Jen wasn't surprised. It was a new burner phone, the fourth one in the last two weeks.

"Hi Mom, it's me, your wayward daughter and trouble maker extraordinaire," she joked.

"I tried to call you last night, I was worried when I couldn't get a hold of you." The stress in her voice came across loud and clear. Guilt ate at Jen for that and so much more.

"I'm sorry, Mom. I lost it yesterday morning and didn't have a chance to buy a new one until today. I'm fine, I promise," Jen replied and swore to tell her everything once she got home. After she put distance between her and the nightmare she'd been living

"It's okay, sweetheart. But what's really going on? I wasn't born yesterday. No one loses phones as often as you have lately unless there's a problem."

"I'm okay," Jen said, twirling her long blonde hair around her index finger. It was a nervous habit Kurt had tried to break. "We can talk about it when I get there. I was thinking of coming home for a visit." Holding her breath, she hoped she wouldn't ask more questions she couldn't answer.

"You are? It's been so long, I'd love it. When do you think you'll come? I've missed seeing your beautiful face so much."

"How about tomorrow? I would probably get in after dinner sometime. If that's okay?" Jen had a lot to be sorry for when it came to her mom. For the past year, Kurt had controlled every aspect of her life. Her mom would be devastated if she knew. Or worse, would try to do something about it. "I'll get the train to D.C. in the morning and the connecting one to Norfolk. If I'm lucky, I'll get there in time for a late dinner."

"Really? Tomorrow? I'd love it. Do you want me to pick you up at the station?"

"I'll grab a taxi. You have enough to do with the bar. I'm thirty-two years old, I can find my way home." Relief flooded her body, easing tension in her shoulders and neck. She didn't realize how tight she held the phone until her mom said she could go back home. Tears filled her eyes. She had a way out. How did it get this bad?

"Okay. But are you sure there's nothing I need to know? My mom antennae are going off."

Jen chuckled, it had been something she'd dealt with her entire life, and they'd never let her mother down. It would be impossible not to tell her the whole story when they were face-to-face.

"I promise, we'll discuss it when I get home. Okay?"

"Is Kurt coming too?"

The innocent question made Jen's stomach turn over and saliva pool in her mouth. Only over her dead body. No Kurt would not meet her mother if she had any control over it. Ever.

"Nope, just me. Now I need to go and get ready for the trip. I'm sure you're busy at the bar. I'll see you tomorrow, okay?"

"I'm so excited to see you, baby girl. Safe travels. I love you to the moon and back," Pam answered.

"I love you too, Mom. I'm sorry I can't tell you more. At least not yet. See you tomorrow," Jen said as she hung up while fighting back tears. Telling her mother what an ass she'd been would be hard but seeing the hurt in her eyes would tear her apart.

Jen hadn't told her mom how Kurt Walker treated her over the last eight months. No one else believed her when she tried to get help. It would have destroyed her if her mom hadn't either.

The bastard was too good at covering his true nature. Always with a dazzling smile on his face, no one bothered to look close enough to see it never reached his eyes. Why would they? Between his devastatingly handsome good looks and scintillating personality, he was virtually impossible to resist.

Shaking off the fear curdling the coffee she'd had earlier, Jen had to get her ass in gear. She had a lot to accomplish before she could hop the train out of town tomorrow. She'd had a running list she'd kept hidden in her wallet behind her ID card. It was one of the few places she'd known it would be safe.

After weeks of planning, she was ready. All she had to wait for was her opening. She'd gotten it when he'd gotten notification of a large delivery and Kurt had to let them in. That's when she took her chance.

Grabbing her 'go bag' and the plastic zipped bag of money and her journals from the back of the toilet, she snuck out. Convinced he'd catch her at any moment, her heart almost beat out of her chest as she made her way down the stairway. The elevator would have been too risky. When she stepped outside for the first time in three weeks, the overwhelming sense of relief almost brought her to her knees. She'd done it. Or at least step one. Now she had to put distance between them.

Step two was getting on the subway and changing routes two or three times. With each train change, she'd put on a different sweater or top making sure she kept her long blonde hair covered. To be on the safe side, she ended up switching five times before stopping in Queens and checking into the first motel she found.

Three days later she moved to the Voyager

Motel. It was cleaner than the first one, but she wouldn't be sorry to check out in the morning. Every moment since escaping from Kurt's apartment, Jen relaxed a little more. So far she'd kept under the radar, but it wouldn't be long before someone recognized her. The asshole reported her missing and even went to the news stations. Not that she should be surprised. Control was the name of his game.

While she'd been reviewing her escape plan, she heard her name on television. She was in denial as she continued to listen to the lying son-of-a-bitch plead for her return. Her throat closed up and she couldn't breathe as the ramification of what he'd done sank in. She'd barely made it to the bathroom before she puked her entire dinner.

She prayed that the report was only local, at least until she could get home and explain everything to her mother. But now, she'd have to be even more careful.

Tomorrow she'd put more distance between them if everything went according to plan. But first, she needed the supplies to change her appearance. Tucking her hair under a baseball hat and grabbing her coat, made her way outside and into the rain. As she hurried past the crowds on her way to the store, goose-bumps popped up all along her skin and her teeth chattered. The cold raindrops slid down her face and neck like icy fingers reminding her of Kurt.

By the time Jen reached the drug store a few blocks away, she was soaked, ice-cold, and second-guessing her decision to go home. Kurt was a lawyer for a big Manhattan firm and had lots of influential friends. He'd made sure to introduce her to most of them, and they either didn't realize or didn't care he was a monster. What if he used them to track her down? Would he hurt her mother too?

Still shivering as she stood in line at the checkout with the boxes of hair color and a pair of scissors and some rubber gloves, she just wanted to get back to her room. When she was done with her little beauty project, she doubted anyone would recognize her.

He'd already tracked her down once. That's what she got for bringing the phone he'd given her. She'd changed motels and bought a bunch of burner phones to switch every few days. So far it had worked, and after tomorrow she wouldn't have to worry about it, she'd be home and hopefully permanently out of his reach.

Getting out of New York was the only option she could come up with that gave her any chance to be free. Tomorrow was D-day as in disappear day. Jen Turner would no longer exist, and Sky Russell would take her place at least for a while.

After taking a couple of wrong turns, Jen found the used clothing store the clerk at the drug store told her about. The goal was to change her look and after searching through the clothing racks it wouldn't be hard. She was more of a classical "book worm" style, but Jen needed to disappear, at least for the short-term.

Finding out she could trade at least some of her clothing made it even better. He'd know she was there if he saw her clothes on the racks, but the odds were in her favor. Picking out a couple of pairs of shredded and faded jeans, t-shirts in assorted colors and snarky sayings, she was almost done. There were two things she still needed, and finally, in the back of the store, she found them. An old navy blue peacoat and high-top sneakers. Jen wasn't thrilled about wearing someone else's shoes, but they were in excellent condition and keeping her fancy boots would be a dead giveaway.

The clerk happily took her designer clothing, courtesy of the asshat—especially the leather boots—and she only owed ten dollars for everything. Knowing how much the boots cost, she probably should have gotten all of her selections for free, but she didn't really care.

It was transformation time. In the dressing room, Jen took off the clothing from her life with Kurt. It was a metamorphosis like a caterpillar to a butterfly and considering her new hair color it fit. She carefully folded her clothes to turn over to the cashier, and she pulled on the snarkiest t-shirt from the ones she'd picked out and couldn't help smiling. The torn jeans fit like a glove. They were two sizes smaller than the last pair she'd bought before Kurt. She'd lost so much weight most of her curves were gone.

Dragging off the boots and slipping on the Chucks she was almost ready. Pulling off the baseball hat, she shook out her hair. After her beauty night, her hair was a lot shorter, only about shoulder length instead of almost to her ass. But the biggest change was the color which was now a combination of blue and pink. If that didn't throw Kurt off, nothing would.

As she approached the front counter to hand over the rest of her clothing to the clerk, she did a double-take.

"If I hadn't seen you buy that stuff, I'd never know it was you. You going to some kind of party or something?"

Jen smiled to herself. It was the reaction she'd hoped for. "Yeah, something like that. Thanks for your help."

"Come back anytime."

"I will," Jen said as she stepped through the door. It was one more white lie to add to her list. Next stop Penn Station and her great escape.

Waiting in line at the ticket window, she kept expecting Kurt to show up and grab her by the arm and drag her off, threatening her if she made a sound. There was also the chance that someone would have seen her on TV and recognized her. But she'd been lucky so far. Her next hurdle was buying the ticket. By law, she needed to present her ID. If the person on the other side of the window recognized her name she'd be in deep shit.

The line moved slowly, it was mid-morning and busy in the terminal. Finally, she was the next in line. Anxious she'd be discovered, sweat broke out on the back of her neck, and her hands shook as she handed over her license and money for the ticket. She was prepared to run if the worst happened.

The ticket dude didn't even look at her, just printed the ticket and handed her back her ID, the ticket and change. Breathing a sigh of relief, she double-checked that her ticket was for the ten a.m. train to Washington, D.C. With time to kill before she needed to be on the platform, she stopped at one of the kiosks and bought a couple of bottles of water and snacks.

The trip took a few hours and even though she wasn't hungry now, she would be. Looking over her shoulder and checking her surroundings had become second nature for her and she hated the feeling she was being watched. It wouldn't surprise her at all for Kurt to hire someone to find her, but they'd be looking for a blonde-haired Jen, not Sky with the blue and pink hair.

As the train pulled up to the platform, Jen took a deep breath. Going back home to escape a lunatic boyfriend wasn't part of her life plan, but if it worked she could start over. After climbing onto the train, she walked through a couple of cars before she took an empty seat by the window. Before sitting down she stowed her backpack on the rack above her head but kept her oversized tote with her. With each passing moment her tension eased, and the stiffness in her neck and tightness in her shoulders relaxed. Not that she was totally in the clear yet, but it was getting closer. For the first time in months, her stomach stopped its flips and churning enough acid to melt steel.

The wheels squealed as they departed the Penn Station and she closed her eyes and said a silent prayer as a single tear slid down her cheek. It was a non-stop to D.C. and the railcar she'd chosen was about two-thirds full. The seat next to her had remained empty and she put her tote beside her. She'd done it. After two weeks of hiding in the city, she was on her way to freedom from the psychotic bastard who'd tried to enslave her. When it came right down to it, she couldn't look at it any other way.

When talking about her past she'd always been vague and couldn't be more thankful for that now. Even if he did figure out where she was from, would it be worth his while to follow her so far away? There were so many women in New York, he probably had a list to choose from. Not that she'd wish him on anyone.

CHAPTER 3

Waking up at zero dark thirty didn't bother Murph. After eight years in spec ops, it was just part of his routine. But he had to admit, the first morning after returning from a mission and getting to sleep in his own bed made it less desirable. Not bothering with a shower since he was meeting the guys for a ten-mile run, he headed to the kitchen to make coffee.

While waiting for the coffee to brew, he turned on the TV to see what he'd missed over the last two weeks. After the typical political back and forth by the talking heads, they went on to the regular news. There were two police officers shot in New York, a workplace stabbing in Florida, and more kids arrested for attempted school shootings. What the fuck was wrong with the world?

The more they tried to protect America, the more it destroyed itself from the inside. Deciding he'd had enough bad news for one morning, he picked up the remote to turn off the TV when a woman's face appeared on the screen. She seemed familiar, but he didn't remember meeting her. He couldn't pull his eyes away from the TV. It wasn't just her long blonde hair and pretty face, there was something about her expression and the light in her emerald eyes. He was so focused on her that he didn't hear what the newscaster said, and he had to rewind it to hear the report. The woman named Jennifer Turner was missing for over a week from the apartment she shared with Kurt Walker in Tribeca. Then they flashed a photo of Walker on the screen since he'd been the one to report her disappearance.

Looking into the man's eyes made Murph's skin crawl. They were cold, not worried, not remorseful, or even shining with love. From his experience, someone like that was never a good guy and he hoped the police took a good look at him. Unfortunately, the odds weren't in the woman's favor if she'd been missing that long.

Shaking off the feeling he knew her, he poured a cup of coffee, downed it, and then filled his travel mug to take with him. After adding a couple of water bottles to his workout bag, he headed out the door to start the day.

As he climbed into his truck his cell rang. Tossing the bag on the passenger seat, he pulled the phone out of his sweatshirt pocket and checked the caller ID.

"Hey, Jake. What's up?"

"Head to Base. There's been a development."

"Copy that. I'm on my way. Do you want me to call anyone?"

"Already taken care of, but thanks."

The first few days after returning from a mission were usually just light duty, mostly just PT and any extra debriefing that might be needed. If they were being called in, something major happened. Murph hoped that they'd gotten a good location for Azfaar and they could finally put an end to that twat waffle once and for all. Maybe that's what Jake and the captain were talking about yesterday after the debriefing. Although, it was weird to wait until this morning to tell the rest of the team.

Everyone else except for Jake was waiting in the parking lot for him. Pulling into his usual spot, he jumped out with his coffee.

"Morning." Murph joined his teammates and patted Halo on the head.

"Morning," the guys responded almost at the same time.

"Anyone know what's going on?"

"Not yet. I guess we'll find out soon enough. Since the captain is here too it could be news about Azfaar," Rafe answered.

"I really hope it's that douche canoe, he's way overextended his life span," Murph remarked as they headed into the building.

"Agreed," Ryan replied. "Now go put on your uniform, Murph, so we can get in there before we get our asses chewed."

There wasn't one member of the Black Eagles that didn't want Azfaar's head on a plate. He'd done more than enough damage to their team individually and the rest of the world even though most people never heard of him. If they'd found him, Murph would be happier than a pig in mud to head out after him.

The conference room was almost full by the time the SEALs entered. Murph and Ryan exchanged glances. This had to be something bigger than Azfaar since not only was Captain Knox there but also the assistant director of the CIA, and Mark Wood from Homeland Security. With all the alphabets except the FBI in the room, Murph stowed his snarky greeting and took a seat at the conference table with the rest of his team.

The moment they were told to take their seats, and then the door opened, as the Red Falcon team filed in. They gave Murph's team a chin lift in greeting and then stood at ease in the back of the room. The last time the conference room had been this packed was when they were being sent out after Osama Bin Laden. SEAL Team Six did the actual takedown but they'd been on standby for back up if needed.

Captain Knox stepped up to the podium and looked around the room. Apparently satisfied with what he saw, he started speaking.

"As I'm sure you've figured out by now, we have a situation. It's still in the early stages. The

CIA and Homeland Security uncovered a plot by Iran to take out Bagram. The intel is still fluid and until we have further confirmation you're on standby. It may happen today, tomorrow, or the Deltas on site might be able to neutralize without assistance. If you don't know Mark Wood, he's our Homeland liaison, and I'll let him take over. Save the questions for the end."

Jake and his counterpart on the Red Falcon team, Quinn Gallagher, exchanged looks and then turned back to face the podium. Murph wondered if there was something else in play that they weren't telling the teams.

"I think most of you already know me but in case you don't, I took over for Gene Arnold. Before working at Homeland Security, I was Army spec ops, so I know the shit you have to deal with from the recent cases of bad intel affecting your missions."

The low murmur of surprise and agreement around the room confirmed his words.

"That's why we're not heading out yet. I want to make sure we have as much confirmed as possible. As Captain Knox said, the intel is very fluid and could be just a lot of BS in response to the POTUS. With the recent rocket launches and injuries to our fellow soldiers, we aren't going to take this lightly, you have my promise."

"What we do know has been put together by Chrissy Stillwell and she'll run you through it here shortly. We can't afford any mistakes. We sure as fuck don't want to go into Iran if we're wrong," Assistant Director of the CIA, Ralph Cummings, stressed. "It would be a clusterfuck of epic proportions."

Another murmur of consent made its way around the room.

Captain Knox stepped back to the mic. "Any questions for Assistant Director Cummings or Mark? If not I'll have Chrissy get to the intel we do have."

The room remained silent. Murphy never understood why they asked for questions halfway through. What was the point until they knew more details? He thought it was interesting that Chrissy hadn't shared any of the intel with Ryan, especially since they lived together. It had to make it hell on a relationship.

Turning down the lights, Chrissy shared her computer screen onto the whiteboard.

"This is all we have so far. Our informant has been working undercover for years as part of the

Iranian Ministry of Defense. But he's still not privy to their plans—usually."

"So how do we know this is at all credible? Maybe he's just trying to make a name for himself?" Quinn the boss of the Red Falcon team asked.

Murph thought about the same thing, it wouldn't be the first time. Although if he'd really been in deep cover for so long, maybe he'd turned.

"We don't and that's why you're not wheels up. But we do have others working on verifying the information. As the assistant director said, we don't need to go into Iran with guns blazing and start a new war."

"Do we have anything confirmed?" Jake asked.

"Only that if they are planning it that they have the capability, as seen from their recent attacks on American bases. We've heard chatter about the Taliban and Iran working together."

"I guess the peace talks are just bullshit then," Cam remarked.

"I'm not saying that. There's no definitive proof that they're in bed together, but honestly it sure as hell looks like it. Until we have proof, you'll be on standby."

When Chrissy finished going over the rest of the slides, identifying the main actors and locations, the teams had a few more questions. There was so much unknown it made it difficult.

"I'll let you in on this, the White House is taking this as a serious threat. Which means we are. All leave is canceled, and you need to be ready for wheels up at any moment. I'd say as soon as we get any kind of confirmation, we'll be heading out."

Jen concentrated on getting every detail written in her journal. Feeling safer than she had in too long, she couldn't shake the feeling that Kurt was right behind her. If this escape act worked, it would probably take a long time before she stopped looking over her shoulder.

The conductor went through the railcars checking everyone's tickets and when he got to her and asked for her ticket and license, that same foreboding twisted in her gut. But he just punched the ticket and handed everything to her and moved on. One more hurdle overcome.

The last time Jen visited her mother was two months after she'd moved to Soho, and that was at least eight months ago. The one time she'd started planning a trip, Kurt told her he was too busy at work. She'd have preferred to go alone, even though things were still mostly fine then, but he refused. The signs were there, but she never noticed them.

As she put away her license and ticket, her phone vibrated in her bag. Checking the ID, she smiled seeing it was her mom.

Mom: Are you on the way?

Me: Yes, I should get into D.C. around 1.

Mom: Are you okay? On TV they said Kurt reported you missing.

Me: Don't worry, Mom. I'll explain it all when I get home. I promise, I'm okay.

Mom: Please be careful. I love you.

Me: I will, I promise. I'll text you when I know what time the Norfolk train gets in.

Mom: Are you sure you don't want me to pick you up?

Me: I'll just grab a taxi. You have enough with the bar.

Mom: *I can't wait to see you.*

Me: *Me too. Oh and I kind of changed my hair a little bit.*

Mom: *Because of Kurt?*

Me: *Yeah, it's kind of colorful now. It's a surprise.*

It sure was a surprise. Her mom would probably shit when she saw her. But it'd be even harder to explain why she had to pretend to be someone else.

Mom: *Okay. Keep me updated. I can't stop worrying now. And I can't wait to hug you.*

Me: *Just a few more hours. Love you.*

Mom: *I love you.*

The train wouldn't arrive in D.C. for about another hour. As exhausted as she was, Jen couldn't sleep surrounded by strangers. Her skin crawled with worry that Kurt would find her and drag her back to his apartment. Sleep would have to wait until she got home. Instead, she packed her journal into her tote bag and pulled out one of the books she'd purchased at the bookstore when she'd worked there.

It had been a perfect job, she loved reading and writing and hoped one day to have the time to write a book. But Kurt made her quit when he didn't trust she wasn't flirting with the other customers. It had been an awful scene. Jen had been dressed and putting her coat on when he asked her where she was going.

"To work, like always. I'll be home around five-thirty, I think."

I don't think so," Kurt snapped.

"You don't think so what? I don't understand."

"I make plenty of money to support you. You don't need to work anymore."

"But I like working in the bookstore. And Lila is a great boss."

"It doesn't matter, it's done. I called her while you were in the shower and told her you wouldn't be coming in anymore."

"Why the hell would you do that?" It was the first time Jen raised her voice at him, but she was livid. She'd moved into his place a month ago and had been wondering if she'd made a mistake. Who the fuck was he to tell her what she could and couldn't do?

"Watch your tone, Jennifer. I told you that I'd be taking care of you. I meant it. Now go put on some casual clothing and we'll have breakfast together."

At first, she stood plastered to the floor, dumbfounded by what happened, but snapped out of it when he took a step toward her with menace hardening his blue eyes into hard rocks.

"Okay." She stammered the word more than spoke it and ran into the master bedroom and burst into tears of fear and frustration. It was the first time she'd been afraid of him, but it wouldn't be the last.

Concentration eluded her as she sightlessly flipped through the pages of her favorite book. Jen sat up in her seat and looked around. No one new entered the car during the trip at least. They'd be in D.C. soon, time for her to change into something new.

At the used clothing store she'd also bought a couple of wigs. With the bright pink and blue hair, she'd stand out in a crowd on video if anyone checked. To try to throw him off the track if he was looking, the black-haired pixie wig and a new t-shirt should help.

Changing in the bathroom wasn't easy with the jarring of the tracking and the dim light but she managed and returned to her seat looking like a new woman. None of the other riders paid any attention and when they pulled into Union Station. She got off the train and headed to the main concourse to buy her ticket to Norfolk.

Excitement sizzled along her nerve endings. In another four or five hours, Jen would walk straight into her mother's arms and not let go as she inhaled her familiar scent of gardenia. How she'd managed that working in a bar all day was one of her best-kept secrets. Maybe now that she was grown up, her mom would finally tell her.

CHAPTER 4

The Norfolk train had to be moving in slow motion. There was no way they were going seventy miles per hour. Now that Jen was so close to home she could almost reach out and touch it. But she couldn't. Three and a half hours. That's how much longer she had to wait. She didn't know whether she was more excited or nervous about finally getting there.

There had been a two-hour wait for the train before she could leave D.C. after the almost three-hour train ride. It would have been so much easier and faster if she'd rented a car, but too much of a trail to leave for Kurt. Maybe she was overreacting to the whole thing, but after seeing her face plastered on TV, she didn't think so.

It was the last leg of the trip, soon she'd be home. But she'd also have to explain almost everything to her mom. Especially that she had to call her Sky and not Jen.

Me: I'm on the Norfolk train. Finally, be there in about 3.5 hours.

Mom: Are you still doing okay? No trouble?

Me: No trouble. This train is fairly empty, and I've got my own seat..

Mom: Good. You have enough problems without having to deal with a weirdo on the train.

Me: When you see me, besides the change in how I look, I'm going to use the name Sky Russell for a bit.

Mom: What? Why? What the hell is going on?.

Jen cringed. Her mom never cursed.

Me: He's looking for me. It will make sense when I can explain everything after I get home. But to keep it easy I figured I'd use your maiden name. I'll be Amanda's daughter, your old made-up friend. And I doubt anyone knows my middle name is Skylar. It seemed the easiest way to remember.

She could imagine the look on her mom's face, staring at her phone and wondering what the hell was wrong with her. It seemed to take forever before she replied, but it was really less than a minute.

Mom: *Why didn't you call me? I don't like this. I'm going to need a double to get through your explanation, aren't I?*

Me: *A double tea?*

Her mom never drank, not even on holidays. Jen didn't have any idea why, but she thought it was kind of ironic that a teetotaler owned a bar.

Mom: *With extra cookies.*

That sounded more like her mom.

Me: *I promise, it'll make sense later. See you in a few hours.*

Mom: *Be safe, Jen.*

Mom: *I mean Sky. This is not going to be easy.*

Me: *I'm sorry. Love you.*

Mom: *Love you more.*

Me: *Don't forget to delete the text messages.*

Mom: *I won't. See you soon.*

It was strange reading it but hearing it and remembering to respond would take some getting used to. Too bad she didn't have the time. Keeping her real identity hidden needed to happen. If Kurt found her she didn't know what he'd do, and now that he'd involved the police she might be in trouble too. He could charge her with theft for taking her clothing. Who knew what he'd try at this point.

The tightness in her shoulders extended into her neck until just turning to look out the window brought tears to her eyes. Had she made a huge mistake going home and getting her mom involved?

As the train neared the station, Jen once again got up and changed her look. This time it was a new snarky t-shirt and no wig. Finger fluffing her hair in front of the small mirror, she got it almost presentable, but good enough to be able to get a taxi. If not she'd have to call her mom to come and get her.

The trip seemed to take forever. By the time the train rolled into the station her butt was sore and her legs were stiff, and she almost took a header down the steps to the platform. If the conductor hadn't grabbed hold of her arm she'd have fallen flat on her face. Black eyes and a broken nose probably would have helped hide her identity but what a fucked up way to do it. It *almost* made her chuckle.

"Thank you." Jen smiled as she slid the backpack over one shoulder and the tote bag over the other.

"You're welcome, young lady. Have a good evening," the elderly conductor replied.

After another smile she walked across the platform to the terminal, thinking how much the conductor looked like Mr. Conductor from Thomas the Tank Engine. Thankfully, it wasn't crowded since it was after rush hour and even found a taxi waiting in front of the terminal. It wouldn't be long now until she could hug her mom. So close to feeling safe for the first time in forever. So close to finally sleeping for more than an hour or two at a time.

Stepping outside into the evening air and the smell of the ocean, it was already dark at seven p.m. She'd been traveling since ten a.m. It would only be another ten minutes or so until she arrived at the Ready Room and would see Mom. Hopefully, most of the dinner hour would be over, not that they served a lot, mostly standard bar food, sandwiches, burgers, fries, nachos. Just thinking about it made Jen's stomach growl. She shouldn't be surprised since all she'd eaten was a granola bar while waiting to hop on the Norfolk train.

It wouldn't be long until she was home and this nightmare will be over. As she watched the familiar surroundings through the window, her excitement grew. Soon she'd be able to hug her mother, sleep in her old bed, and not wake up terrified for the first time in months. Kurt cut her off from everyone, controlling every moment of every day, leaving her scared and alone.

"Here you go, the Ready Room."

It still looked the same, like some dive bar, except it was always filled with regulars, mostly from the naval base. She remembered the regular crowd and how it would shift all the time with military moves and deployments. Would the regulars still be here? If they were, there's a chance they'd recognize her. Keeping her identity a secret was going to be a lot harder than she thought. Coming back home was probably not the wisest decision when she was trying to hide.

Grabbing her backpack and tote, she climbed out of the backseat and paid the taxi driver. Standing outside the building she'd called home for most of her life, she took a deep breath, hoping to settle the butterflies in her stomach.

Shit. She hadn't thought about how odd it would look for her to walk into the bar with all of her stuff. Maybe she should go around back and text her mom. Before she could decide, she heard someone come up behind her. Terrified it was Kurt, she spun around ready to do whatever she needed to keep him from grabbing her.

"Easy. I'm not going to hurt you. I'm sorry I startled you." The man said as he took a step back and held his hands up with his palms facing her.

Forcing herself to focus on him and not the fear coursing through her body, it definitely wasn't Kurt. Where he was a blond, blue-eyed pretty boy, this man was tall, dark-haired, and could have been a cover model for Men's Health. Her breathing slowly returned to normal and her heart stopped pounding out of her chest.

"No, I'm sorry. I shouldn't have been blocking the door." Jen was surprised her voice sounded normal.

"Are you sure you're okay? Maybe you should go inside and sit down." His deep voice had a slight southern drawl. The hard, chiseled lines of his face eased as he smiled, and his eyes glinted from the street lights.

"I'm okay. I'm new to Norfolk. My mom is from here and I'm here to see her friend. But now I'm not so sure. It looks a little rough."

Making shit up as she went along, her mother would kill her if she heard her precious bar described as a dive.

"Only on the outside. It's a great place. Let's see if we can find your mom's friend. Are you sure she still works here?" He reached around her, and she backed away, she hadn't meant to, it was pure instinct. He frowned but didn't say anything.

"Thank you."

As he pulled open the door, the aroma of burgers and beer made her mouth water. But it was Gloria Gaynor's voice singing '*I will survive*' playing on the jukebox that affected her the most. Like it was a sign.

He waited patiently for her to go inside, and her cheeks heated as she realized he was still holding the door open for her.

"You're welcome, ma'am. If you need anything, come and find me. I'll be sitting in the back of the bar with a few of my friends. Oh, and I'm Murph." He reached out to shake her hand, but she couldn't bring herself to touch him. Staring at it, all she could see was Kurt reaching for her and a shiver of fear slid down her spine.

"I'll be fine, but I appreciate your offer. Have a nice night." Jen hated being rude, but it was as polite as she could manage. All the fear and stress as she planned her escape from the loft and then hiding until she was sure it was safe to come home. And hell, she still wasn't sure it was really safe. How she hadn't had a nervous breakdown she had no idea.

"Thank you. I don't mean to be rude, it's just been a long day," Jen said hoping she didn't sound rude. Hating how much her personality had changed, she hoped that being home and around Mom would help her feel like herself again.

Murph had done nothing but be polite and try to help her. In another time she'd have appreciated his help, but not tonight, maybe not ever. Not until she was safe from the monster who'd covered her in emotional scars.

Surprised at the crowd on a Thursday night, Jen walked further inside and searched for her mother. Not seeing her anywhere, she wove her way around the people and headed for the kitchen. If her mom wasn't behind the bar or serving customers, she was probably grabbing her next order or helping anyone who needed it.

Pam Turner was a great boss and all of her staff loved her.

Jen didn't have to look to know Murph was watching her and when she turned, he had an odd look on his face. If she didn't know better, she'd think he recognized her, But how could he? If she'd met him, there's no way she'd have forgotten Mr. Too Sexy for his Jeans. She may not want to be around men, but she could still appreciate a fine specimen when she saw one.

Freaked out that he was so focused on her, she took a few deep breaths to slow her heartbeat and relax. The last thing she wanted was to be a wreck when she found her mother. The fight or flight reflex was hard to suppress, and even though she told herself that he wasn't a threat believing it was a different story.

As she walked down the short hallway off the main bar area, she heard her mother's laughter coming from the kitchen. They weren't supposed to know each other but all she wanted to do was through herself into her mom's arms and hug her until they couldn't breathe, but that would have to wait until they were alone.

Her mom hadn't really changed since she'd seen her last, maybe a few more grey hairs.

Repeating over and over that she was Sky, she walked into the kitchen. One of the cooks saw her first.

"You're not supposed to be back here," Tony Ramirez said.

He'd worked at the Ready Room for at least ten years and when he didn't recognize her, she let out the breath she'd been holding.

"I'm sorry. I'm looking for Pam Turner?"

Her mom turned at Tony's words and her face lit up when she saw Jen. Thankfully, she remembered they weren't supposed to know each other.

"I'm Pam. Can I help you with something?"

"I'm Sky Russell, Amanda's daughter. She said she was going to call you…" Jen let her voice trail off, trying to sound awkward and unsure.

"Sky. Yes, she did. I'm so happy to meet you. She's told me so much about you over the years. Let's get you upstairs. You're going to stay here, right?"

"If it's not too much trouble. I can get a motel until I can find an apartment."

"No need. You're practically family," her mom said and winked when she knew no one else could see them.

"Thank you, that would be great."

"Tony, I'll be back in a few. Can you ask Sandy to cover my tables for about an hour?"

"Will do, boss."

"C'mon, Sky, after we get you settled, you can come back down and have something to eat."

"Down?"

"Yes, I live upstairs, makes it really convenient."

"I didn't realize," Jen said. This was a lot harder than she thought. How she'd keep up the façade she had no idea.

Following her mother through the rear door and into the back alley, they didn't say anything. As soon as her mom got the door to the hallway to the upstairs apartment open, and they were hidden from everyone, she turned and pulled Jen into her trembling arms.

"I'm so glad you're here. I was so worried after I saw your picture on the television. All the regulars were asking about you."

"I'm sorry." Tears filled Jen's eyes and rolled down her cheeks. It was such a huge mess. If she was missing the police would eventually contact her mom. She was surprised they hadn't already.

This was a huge mess and she'd made it worse by bringing it here. What had she been thinking?

"C'mon, let's get inside and then we can talk."

Jen had been dreaming of this moment, being home, for so long, and the reality was even better. Taking her bags to the guest room, she dropped them on the bed with a sigh of relief. Everything was a big pile of horse poop but for the next few minutes, she was going to enjoy being home. It has been forever since she'd stayed at her mom's.

"I didn't change anything. I'd thought about making it into a craft room. But who was I kidding, when would I have time for that?" Pam said from behind Jen.

"I shouldn't have come. It was selfish of me."

"Of course you should have, this is your home. We'll figure this out."

Jen wrapped her arms around her mom's waist and squeezed. It was the best feeling ever. As they stood wrapped in each other's arms, she was enveloped in the scent of gardenias and the tears she'd held in poured like rain.

CHAPTER 5

As Murph made his way through the crowded bar toward his friends, he tried to recall where he'd seen her before. Until he figured it out, it would drive him crazy. It was one of his 'super-powers' that he never forgot a face, and it aided them on missions more than once. And who goes to a bar with a backpack and a tote?

When he approached her outside the bar he'd thought she was homeless and was going to offer her some money. Then she turned around and the fear in her eyes flipped every protective switch he didn't know he'd had. Years of training kept him from reaching for her. From the look on her face, she'd probably have kneed him in the balls?

Distracted by his interaction with the woman, Murph nodded at his teammates, poured himself a beer from the pitcher already on the table, and sat between Ryan and Rafe. Taking a long swig from his mug, he relaxed into the chair and sighed. First the mission and then reviewing intel all day, now his brain needed a rest.

"What took you so long?" Rafe asked.

"Didn't you see that woman he came in with?" Ryan said and winked at Murph. "She didn't seem your type with all that pink and blue hair. It looked like those popsicles I used to get when I was a kid. What the fuck did they call them?"

"Sky blue pink," Rafe answered.

"Yeah, that's it. Sky blue pink."

Murph just shook his head. The only single guy at the table since Jake hadn't shown up yet, they were going to have their fun. Plus the bet they'd made with him was winding down. Even though the money was going to charity, no way was he going to lose and have to serve them beer in a pink tutu. They were shit out of luck, no matter how much they wanted to see it.

"No, she isn't my type, but there's something

about her. I swear I've met her before, but I can't figure it out."

"*You* can't remember?" Cam asked, obviously surprised. "You never forget a face."

"I know." Murph took another long swig from his beer. "It's going to bug the fuck out of me until I figure it out. She looked so lost. I offered to help, but she blew me off."

"Wait, a woman blew you off? You're losing your touch, Bro." Rafe chuckled.

"Not like that. Shit. You guys suck sometimes. I didn't hit on her. The woman looked terrified when she saw me behind her outside."

"She didn't look familiar to me, but I was distracted by the hair. Do you think she's in trouble?" Ryan asked.

"I don't know. But I can't force her to take my help. There was just something about her eyes though, I've never seen eyes so green, like emeralds. But they were filled with fear. Ugh…" Murph's voice trailed off and sighed again. Damn, he was doing a lot of that lately. Changing the subject, he asked, "Where's Jake?"

"He's coming, said he had to make a call and he'd catch up with us," Rafe replied.

"That's been happening a lot lately. Think he's

okay?" Cam asked absentmindedly rubbed Halo's head as it rested on his thigh.

Maybe he needed to get a dog. Except he'd have to worry about boarding it when they left on missions and he'd hate doing that to an animal. As he listened to his teammates talk about their women, Murph wondered about Ms. Sky Blue Pink. Ryan was right, her hair color was dead on.

"What, no women tonight?" Jake asked as he sat in the last empty chair.

He looked about as tired as Murph felt, and he wondered why they hadn't brought them, it had become the norm.

"We felt sorry for you guys, so we left them home for a girls night at my house," Rafe replied.

"Bullshit, you probably wore them out with all of your squatting in the cucumber patch. I bet they couldn't even stand up."

"Jesus, Murph, where the fuck do you come up with this stuff?" Ryan said after choking on his swallow of beer.

"You didn't have to leave them home on our account," Jake said. "I invited Quinn and his team to join us, but they took a rain check. Probably a good thing, we'd have had to knock some heads together to get more chairs. Is there something going on tonight I don't know about?"

"We were wondering the same thing," Cam said.

"Hey, guys sorry I've been neglecting you. It's a little crazy in here tonight," Pam said as she placed a large bowl of pretzels on their table.

"We were just talking about that. What's going on?" Cam asked.

"A birthday party, at least that's what they told me," Pam replied with a wink and a smile. "You never know with you Navy guys. I'll get these pitchers refilled. Can I get you anything else?"

"How about a couple of orders of chicken wings?" Jake said.

"Extra hot like usual?"

"And some nachos too," Cam chimed in.

Pam laughed. "Sure, anything else?"

"Hey, Pam. Did that girl find you?" Murph asked, carefully watching her reaction. Maybe the Sky Blue Pink had lied to him and she was up to no good.

"What girl?"

"When I got here, there was a girl with pink and blue hair carrying a couple of bags standing in front of the bar. When I asked if she needed help, she said she was looking for you."

"Oh, yeah, she found me. Her name is Sky. She's the daughter of my best friend from high school."

Pam was blinking too much and not making eye contact. A clear sign she wasn't telling the truth or at least not all of it. Murph couldn't shake the feeling there was something wrong.

"That's cool. Is she staying with you?"

"Yes, until she can find a place."

"That explains the bags, then," Murph remarked.

"Is there something you want to ask me, Murph? I feel like I'm getting the third degree."

Rafe kneed him under the table. Shit, he had been kind of grilling her.

"Sorry, I didn't mean to put you on the spot. She looked scared and lost when I saw her. She was probably just nervous about meeting you."

"Gotcha. All right, I'll be right back with your food and more beer."

"What the fuck was that?" Jake asked as he gave Murph the hairy eyeball. "And what did I miss?"

Before Murph could answer, Ryan filled Jake

in on Murph's interaction with Sky earlier. He appeared to really enjoy telling him how she blew him off. Then finished up with his idea that her hair color was like the ice cream and how ironic that her real name was Sky. It was a good thing they were family, the only one he had left, or he'd kick his ass.

"What's bugging you, Murph?" Jake asked.

"I'm not sure. My gut is telling me I know her and that she's in trouble. But I have no idea why."

Jake nodded but didn't say anything at first, just seemed to consider what he'd been told. There was a reason he'd reached the rank of master chief. Calm, cool, and collected didn't even begin to describe him. In all the years Murph knew him, he'd never seen him lose it, no matter how bad shit got, not even after they'd returned home. He was as rock-solid as they got and had a knack for figuring shit out when no one else could. Murph often wondered if after Jake retired he'd go to work for one of the alphabet agencies.

"What do you want to do about it?" Jake asked Murph after a couple of moments.

"I don't have a fucking clue. Keep trying to figure out what's bugging me, I guess."

Jake nodded but didn't respond since Pam was back with their food and more beer.

"I'll be back to check on you in a bit."

Pam's attitude was part of what was bugging him. They'd known her for years, and he couldn't remember a day when Pam wasn't working at the Ready Room. There had been speculation for years that she was the owner, but no one could get her to admit to it. One of the other teams' guys had even looked it up but it was owned by some corporation no one knew anything about.

Murph would bet Tex could figure it out in about ten minutes, but it wasn't worth bothering him over. But Sky was another story, he had no problem contacting him if he couldn't shake the sense of foreboding that caused the little hairs on the back of his neck to tingle.

"Did anyone else get a good look at her?" Jake asked.

"I didn't," Rafe responded.

"I could identify her but as for a good look, not really. I didn't look closely enough for the details, I thought he was just hitting on another woman," Ryan said before shoving an overloaded nacho chip into his mouth.

"Me either, sorry, Boss," Cam said.

Murph watched as he grabbed one of the nacho chips and brushed everything off onto the plate in front of him then fed it to Halo. It made him smile for the first time since getting there that evening. Maybe he was being too intense. Letting his exhaustion and frustration over not catching Azfaar get to him.

He reached for some of the nachos and added a couple of wings on his plate. Then he took the liberty of topping everyone's beer off with the pitcher. These were some of the best wings, and he'd sampled them just about everywhere in the U.S.

"I think, if you can let it go for now, then do it. I'm not telling you to ignore your instincts. But until something happens there's not much we can do now."

"Okay." Murph was frustrated. Just because Jake was right, he didn't have to like it. He'd have to wait and see what happens.

"But, if you still feel strongly about this tomorrow, we'll give Tex a call with the information we have and see what he finds out."

"Copy that."

"Oh and the captain called, after PT in the morning we have more intel to review."

"Are we going?" Cam asked after he swallowed the chicken drumette he'd sucked off the bone in one bite.

"It'll be a toss-up between us and the Red Falcon Team. But I'm not sure they'll send anyone if we can't get a better confirmation."

Nodding in agreement, they ate in companionable silence, until Rafe and Jake fought over the last wing.

"Drop it, it's mine," Jake demanded while he attempted to hide his smile.

"No way, possession is nine-tenths of the law," Rafe said.

"I don't care about possession, I outrank you, sailor, so step away from the wing."

It wasn't the first time this scenario played out, and the odds were even at fifty-fifty. Ryan put a ten-dollar bill on the table, and Cam matched it.

They'd bet on just about anything, but they always donated the winnings to charity. Murph put down his money and took Jake's side. He looked extra determined and he did outrank Rafe.

A couple of the guys from neighboring tables got in on the betting and soon there was a pile of bills in front of Ryan.

"Seriously, you're going to play the rank card? Don't be a dick, can't you see I'm starving here?" Rafe pleaded his case.

It was all in good fun and as others gathered around their table to see how it would play out. Rafe was going down, no way would Jake let him win after that. Just as predicted, Jake reached across the table and snatched the wing off the plate so quickly Rafe never had a chance.

Score one for the boss tonight.

Not sure what made him do it, but he looked up at one of the TVs mounted on the wall just as they flashed a photo of the woman missing from New York City. The one he'd seen the other day. He couldn't hear what the reporter was saying, and the sub-titles weren't on. But then they changed to a picture of Mr. Pretty Boy. He didn't have a clue what he was saying, but then the graphic changed. It was a reward poster offering a fifty-thousand dollar reward for any information leading to the location of Jennifer Turner.

As he focused on the image on the screen it all clicked. He was looking into the same emerald green eyes he'd seen earlier. What the ever-living fuck? The missing woman was in

Norfolk and posing as someone named Sky? It didn't make sense, why come here, why involve Pam? Unless they were related. While the questions raced through his head faster than he could catalog them, a crash came from behind the bar.

It was loud enough that almost every person in the room turned toward the noise. Murph stood so quickly his chair fell backward with a crash. But he didn't care. It was the sight he saw that took his breath away. Staring across the crowded bar, a lightbulb in his brain went off, and he knew exactly why Sky looked so familiar. She was the missing woman, Jennifer Turner. The eyes were unmistakable, but instead of the smiling happy woman in the photo on the TV, her face was a mask of sheer terror. Murph would bet a month's salary that the asshat offering the reward was the one who put it there.

CHAPTER 6

When Jen finally stopped crying, her mom pulled back enough to kiss her face. It was probably red, blotchy, with mascara trails. But her mom's gentle smile filled with love nearly restarted the waterworks.

"I love you," her mom murmured as she pulled Jen into another embrace. "Whatever it takes we'll get through this. I promise. You're home."

They were almost identical in height, but that's where the similarity ended, although some people said she looked just like her mom. Jen had inherited her dad's blond hair and green eyes, where her mom had what she insisted was mousy brown hair and brown eyes. Wrangling her emotions into check, she sighed as she took a step back out of her mom's arms.

"I just pray I haven't brought trouble here. I'll never forgive myself if something happens to you."

"It won't."

"You can't know that. He's devious and conniving and a total dirtbag."

"There was no one you could turn to in New York?" Her mom led her over to the sofa then went into the kitchen to get them water. The apartment was small, and Jen hated it when they first moved there. It was so different from the little house they'd shared with her dad. But as always her mom had been right, it would have been too hard to stay there. They needed a new beginning and it became the only home that mattered.

"You've seen him on TV, right? He's the epitome of suave and debonair."

"That doesn't mean he can't be a bad guy."

"No, it doesn't. But he was wonderful around others. A big shot partner in his law firm, donating to charities, the perfect guy. Until he wasn't." Jen took a drink of water and thought about how to explain without upsetting her mom any more.

"I know that look. Don't even try to fudge the truth. I'll get it out of you eventually and you know it. So you might as well make it easier on both of us."

Jen set the water glass on the coffee table and looked into her mother's eyes. She didn't know how badly she'd cried off her makeup, but probably enough that she'd see the remnants of the black eyes.

"Sweet mother of God. Oh baby, did he do this to you?" Mom slid across the couch and pulled her into another hug, but this time Jen was able to hold back the tears.

"In a way it's good, it was the impetus I needed to run. He was killing me slowly with the mental games and verbal abuse. But when it got physical something inside me woke up."

"Good? There's nothing good about him hurting you but thank the Lord you got away. I should have come to visit you. Something. I'm so sorry you were all alone."

"No, don't you feel guilty." She reached for her mom's hand and squeezed it between hers.

"This is on me. I wanted a new adventure and I made a bad choice."

Tears rolled down her mom's cheeks and it gutted Jen. It had been eighteen years since she'd seen her mom cry. It reminded her of that last, horrible day.

Mom had been in the kitchen making dinner when the doorbell rang. Jen opened it and at fourteen she knew exactly what seeing the two officers in full dress meant. Her mom had yelled from the kitchen asking who it was. Jen couldn't speak. It was like she'd been glued to the floor.

When she hadn't answered, her mom came to the door, still drying her hands with a towel.

"It's okay. Jen. Please come in," she'd said. "We can sit in here."

Jen remembered wondering how she'd kept so calm when their life had just been turned inside out and ripped to shreds. She didn't remember a word they'd said, only sitting on the couch, and squeezing her mom's hand.

After they were done and the door closed behind the two officers, it was like the dam broke. They'd held on to each other, just like now, and cried until there were no tears left.

"But you're my baby. I should have been able to help."

"No, Mom. You didn't know. Before I realized what was happening, it was too late."

"What do you mean?" her mom asked as she wiped the tears from her cheeks.

"He slowly cut me off from everyone I knew once I moved in with him. I was stupid, it was too fast. I knew it. But he knew just which buttons to push to sweep me off my feet. Who moves in with a guy after dating for two months?" Jen asked, but didn't expect an answer. She couldn't believe she'd fallen for his charm so easily.

"It happens. Your father and I got married after dating for three. But times were different then. No one moved in together without getting married. My father would have had a cow."

"But you and dad were amazing, special. I wanted to find that kind of love and he knew it. I talked about you and he used it all against me."

"You're here now. It'll be okay. Like you said, we'll figure something out."

Her mom nodded. "Why don't you get settled, then come downstairs and have something to eat. You had to have missed Tony's burgers."

"Sounds good. Just remember, I'm Sky, not Jen. I know it'll be hard for both of us. Calling you Pam isn't going to be easy to do."

"It'll be weird hearing you call me that too," Mom said and reached out to squeeze Jen's hand. "I wish I didn't have to go back down, but the crowd is pretty rowdy tonight."

"I saw that. It's fine. We'll have plenty of time to talk later. I'm a big girl, I can find my way back downstairs."

"Okay. Don't forget to grab your key from the table by the door, it's in the little drawer."

"I won't."

As her mom stood to leave, Jen gave her another hug. "Thank you, Mom. For everything. I love you."

"I love you too, always will, no matter what."

Jen had been truly blessed with parents like Pam and Adam Turner. Even though she'd been an only child, they never spoiled her. Instead, they'd instilled their values in her from a young age, but they were always wrapped in love. And even though her dad was long gone, deep in her heart she knew he still watched over them. As she thought about it, she wondered if he'd been the one to finally give her the strength to get away from Kurt.

When her stomach growled, it reminded her she'd eaten nothing since the snack she'd had on the train. Time to get her ass in gear so she could sink her teeth into one of Tony's burgers. Neither of them could get him to share the recipe, but whatever he did, they were the best burgers ever. The Ready Room even won an award for the best burger in Norfolk.

The guest room was pretty much like she left it when it used to be hers, before she left for college and moved into her own apartment. Her mom had kept it clean and hung up a few photos of them from when she was younger. Sitting on the bed, she pulled out her new wardrobe and giggled. With her new colorful hair and the second-hand store clothing finds, she doubted anyone would recognize her. If her high school friends could see her now. It was like Jen's psychedelic makeover. But she was banking on it to work.

Refolding the clothing to put in her dresser, she gazed at the large wardrobe. It had been in her room in their house and she'd pleaded with Mom to keep it even though it really was too big for this room. Of course, she'd relented

Memories flooded back of all the times she'd hidden in there playing hide and seek with her dad, and then later after reading *The Lion, the Witch, and the Wardrobe*, she'd pretend she would go to Narnia. Now she wished it would turn into a time machine. She'd go back and say no to Kurt the twat waffle from day one.

Tears threatened to slide down her cheeks, but she shook them off. There'd been enough crying for one day. Getting up, she made quick work of unpacking the rest of her clothes and setting out her new more elaborate makeup on the dresser.

After catching a glimpse of herself in the mirror she burst out laughing. It looked like she was trying to impersonate Alice Cooper. Holy shit. Yeah, that had to be fixed before she could quiet the rumble in her stomach. With the makeup removed, she took a closer look at her face. The black eyes had faded and now looked more like shadows. Concealer had become her best friend. Finally finished, it was time for food. She almost walked out without her key but remembered before she'd managed to lock herself out.

The bar was still crazy busy from the blast of voices that greeted her when she opened the back door. Her mom could be anywhere, waiting tables, in her office, in the kitchen, or even tending bar. Only the long term staff knew she was the owner and she liked to keep it that way.

Checking as she passed the office and seeing it empty, Jen made a beeline for the kitchen.

Tony looked when she walked through the door. "Hey, Sky, right? Pam said you'd be coming for one of my burgers."

"Yeah, I lo... can't wait to try one." Shit, first conversation and she'd almost blown it already.

"I promise, you won't be disappointed. What do you want on it?"

"Umm, what is the usual?" Knowing if she ordered her usual, he'd know she was Jen or at least be suspicious she'd be happy to have it any way he made it.

"Lettuce, tomato, cheddar, pickles, banana peppers, bacon, and my special sauce?"

"Special, hunh? Are you sure you're not McDonald's?"

"Positive, my sauce is so special no one else has the recipe."

"Okay, I'll give it a go."

"You got it. Pam said she'd be behind the bar. I can have one of the servers bring it out to you if you want?"

"That would be great. Thank you."

What was that old adage, "no time like the present?"

Making her way out to the bar, Jen couldn't believe the number of people. She'd bet they were close to capacity. Great for business, but her mom didn't have enough staff scheduled to handle it. Stepping behind the bar, she smiled at her mom who looked relieved to see her. She wasn't sure if it was for help or to know she was okay. Either way, it didn't matter. It felt like old times when she'd tended bar during summer vacation once she'd turned twenty-one.

"Hi. What can I get you?" Jen asked one of the women waiting.

"A martini, extra dry, two olives and no ice. Oh, and Beefeater if you have it. You really need more people working here. I've been waiting for over five freaking minutes."

"I'm sorry you had to wait. I'll have that right

up." Rolling her eyes as she grabbed a martini glass and mixed the drink, she wondered why her mom loved the bar so much. People were freaking rude. The overdressed woman with perfectly coiffed hair was definitely not a regular.

Using a toothpick to stab two olives from the garnish tray, Jen dropped it into the glass and placed it in front of the snooty woman. "That'll be five dollars."

The woman didn't answer, she just left a ten-dollar bill on the bar and walked away without waiting for her change. Did it mean she wanted to run a tab, or had she left the tip after bitching? Working in the bookstore was a lot easier and people were never rude.

Sandy brought Jen's burger to her behind the bar, but it was too busy still for her to stop and eat. It took another fifteen minutes before they'd caught up and the place started to clear out a bit.

With her mouthwatering for the tasty burger, she grabbed the plate from near the register and turned around and caught a glimpse of her face in a reward poster on TV. Horrified, she dropped the plate with her burger and the crash seemed to echo in her brain.

Her mom was there a moment later. "It's okay Jen, go to my office. I'll pick this up and have Tony make you a new one."

Jen couldn't speak, not even to remind her mom that she'd used the wrong name. Horrified and shaking, she ducked out from behind the bar and closed herself in her mom's office.

CHAPTER 7

"What the fuck?"

Murph heard Ryan but didn't stop to answer or even acknowledge his question. Focused on one thing, he wove his way through the crowd as he kept his eye on Pam and Jen, or Sky, or whoever she really was, as they walked down the hallway. He needed to catch up before he lost sight of them. She might not want his help, but if his gut was on target like usual, she sure as hell needed it.

The door to Pam's office was ajar as he approached and listened for a moment before knocking and entering. He had big brass balls going in without waiting for permission, but the fear on Sky's face when she saw the TV was too much for him to ignore.

"Murph, now is definitely not a good time," Pam said as he stepped into her office.

"But I figured out her secret and if I can, it's sure as shit someone else will too."

As his words sank in, Sky's eyes grew wider and filled with unshed tears. "How is that possible? I hardly recognize myself," she demanded.

"Jen, this is Murph, he's one of the members of the Black Eagle Team. You know him."

Pam calling her Jen cemented it for him. He'd been pretty sure she was her daughter, the one who'd worked at the bar in the summers. She was pretty and smart and not for him. Jen was a keeper, not a fuck and chuck.

"When I saw your face outside I knew you looked familiar. It just took me a bit to figure it out."

"Damn, it's not supposed to be like this. I just freaking got here," she ranted.

"Easy, I'm not going to turn you in. For fuck's sake, what kind of a man do you think I am?"

"I have no idea. You could be just like the douche canoe who offered a reward for information. Hell, maybe you need the fifty thousand. That's the thing, I have no idea who you are."

"Your mother just told you. I've known you or of you for over ten years. I'm a Navy SEAL, and I would never, ever, be a what did you call him? Douche canoe?"

"Sorry, if I won't take you at your word. I've learned my lesson."

"Jen, I know him. He's telling you the truth. Please, sit down and breathe before you pass out," Pam pleaded.

There was another knock on the door, and Pam turned in frustration. "What is going on?"

The door opened to reveal the rest of the team. He should have known they'd follow him. First, because they all loved Pam, and second because of the way he'd charged across the room.

"Sorry, Pam, but Murph took off like a bat out of hell and we didn't know what he'd seen. Someone want to tell us what *is* going on?" Jake asked.

Jen looked up. Murph turned around to see what she saw, which would be four heads trying to peer around the door. Then Halo walked right past him and laid his head on her thigh. Leave it to the dog to solve everything.

Her face melted as she patted the dog's head. "If I tell you, will you all just leave us alone?"

"I can't make that promise," Murph replied. The others agreed. Thank goodness for Halo, or she might have totally come unglued. He'd been around enough people at the end of their rope to recognize desperation when he saw it.

"Jen, listen to me. These are the good guys. Of all the teams that come in here, I'd trust them the most. Maybe they can help?"

After a few seconds, Jen nodded. He moved to make room in the small office for his brothers-in-arms. Ryan was last and closed the door behind him. Surprised that she stayed calm with the amount of testosterone that entered the room, Murph didn't know if she was in shock or just worn down.

"How about I tell you what I think I know, and you can fill in or correct me, that might be easier?" Murph was pretty sure he had it figured out between her reaction and what he'd heard reported on the news.

Jen nodded and Pam mouthed the words thank you.

"Guys meet Jennifer Turner. She's Pam's

daughter. I didn't remember her at first, but she used to work here on her college vacations.

The murmur from behind him acknowledged they remembered.

"From what I've seen on TV, Jen ran away from her boyfriend in New York and is hiding here in Norfolk with her mom. Besides the fact that the guy comes across as a total dirtbag, I'm not sure why the elaborate ruse. Am I close?"

Jen looked surprised and nodded.

"Want to fill us in on the rest?" Murph softened his voice and took a step closer.

As soon as he did, she scooted her chair further away. What the fuck had that guy done to her?

Terrified she was, but there was a spine of steel in there somewhere. Her emerald eyes glistened with tears, but she sat up straighter in the chair and nodded.

"You're right, I'm Pam's daughter and I'm hiding from the guy on television who is an abusive controlling piece of shit but pretends to be a devoted boyfriend in front of the world. I moved to New York City about a year ago, met him shortly after that and he convinced me to move in with him. Yes, I know I was stupid. One of those women I hate that if you hear their story you want to tell them to snap out of it."

"It's okay, honey." Pam reached down and squeezed her hand.

"Anyway, after I moved in he became more and more controlling. Along with that came the verbal abuse. On top of that, he'd play games with me mentally until I didn't know what I was doing." She stopped to take a deep breath.

"Do you want anything to drink?" Murph asked softly.

"Yes, please."

Looking over his shoulder he nodded, and Ryan left to get her some water.

"Go on."

"I tried to talk to my coworkers about him, but no one believed me. They thought I was overreacting. He was handsome, rich, and appeared totally devoted to me. But it was only in public. In private he turned into a monster."

Returning with a bottle of water, Ryan handed it to Murph. He met her eyes and waited a moment before taking a step forward. This time she didn't pull back and reached out to take the bottle from him. What he didn't expect was the sizzle of electricity that ran up his arm as their fingers touched. Taken by surprise, he looked at his fingers and then her face. From the look of disbelief on her face, she'd felt the same thing.

After a moment, she unscrewed the cap and took a drink, then continued. "It was about two months after I moved in with him that he made me quit my job. He said I needed to be home to keep the loft clean and entertain his law partners and clients. It was my new job."

Murph had a pretty good idea where this was going, but he kept his mouth shut to let her finish telling her story. Now that she'd started, it was tumbling out.

"He'd come home at night and walk through the loft. Nothing was allowed to be out of place. Dinner had to be ready a half-hour after he got home so he'd have time to check everything and take a shower before we ate."

"How did you know what time he'd get home?" Rafe asked.

"He'd call me when he was leaving the office. He had a driver bring him from midtown to Tribeca. Then he'd call along the way. I had to wait for him near the door so I could take his briefcase and coat, if he was wearing one, and hang it up in the closet."

"Fucking A," Cam whispered. Murph heard him, but he doubted that Jen did.

"If anything wasn't perfect I'd have to sit on the couch while he berated me until he was satisfied I understood how he wanted things and then send me to bed."

"So, let me get this straight. He basically kept you hostage in his loft and dictated every moment of every day?" Jake asked.

"Yes, exactly. He'd lock me in so I couldn't leave. There was no phone except the cell he'd given me that could only receive calls. I tried and tried to figure out how to unlock it."

A soft noise caught Murph's attention. Pam had gasped and covered her mouth. Obviously, this is the first she was hearing most if not all of this.

"Whenever we were around others he was the perfect boyfriend. No one would believe the hell I lived in."

"If he kept you locked in, how did you get away?" Jake asked before Murph had a chance. Because the dirtbag hadn't let her go if he was offering a reward for information.

"I didn't even try for months. But one afternoon I fell asleep after being up all night and dinner wasn't ready on time. He went berserk and totally lost it. Dumped the dining room table over, sending the dishes and silverware flying. Then he turned toward me. I'd never seen him so mad. I backed away as he approached but then he grabbed me."

The color drained out of her face, but she kept talking.

"I thought he would just scream at me to clean up the mess, but he smashed my face against the wall. Then before I could do anything he punched me in the stomach. I fell on the floor. I couldn't breathe, and that's when he kicked me. I thought for sure he was going to kill me, but he didn't. Without another word he turned and left the loft."

"He just left you like that?" Pam asked with tears on her cheeks.

Murph couldn't imagine the pain she must be going through hearing how the man had terrorized her daughter. He was furious and would like nothing more than to drive up there and beat the shit out of the guy. He'd teach him to touch women or anyone weaker than him.

"What happened next," Murph asked, encouraging her to get it all out.

"I laid on the floor for a while. The pain was incredible, and I didn't know if anything was broken. I'm not sure how long I stayed on the floor, but knowing if I left the mess he'd made, it would be worse for me when he returned. I cleared all the broken dishes and tossed the food, then put the furniture back in its place. I'd just finished when he returned."

"What did he do?" Ryan asked.

"Nothing, absolutely nothing. He acted as if nothing had happened. He came over and kissed me on the cheek and asked what was for dinner. Thankfully, it hadn't been ruined or I don't know what he would have done."

"What happened after that night? Did he threaten you again?" Jake asked.

"It's like he realized he went too far. He was nicer for a bit, but I was never going to let him hurt me again and I started making plans. Trying to come up with some way to get out of there. My break came when a customer sent him a gift that had to be delivered to the house. He had to stay home to accept it since he would keep me locked in."

"What if there was a fire?"

"I don't know, I never thought about it. I guess I would have been toast." When she grinned at her little joke, Murph was shocked. After sitting there telling them everything for the last half hour that she could smile about anything.

"The hardest part was keeping calm, so I wouldn't tip him off. I had only a couple of things I wanted to take with me, and they fit in my purse. He had cameras up all over the house, except the bathroom, so I'd put everything in a zipped bag and taped it inside the toilet. When it was time, I just grabbed the bag and shoved it in my purse."

"How did you actually get out though? He was there with the delivery guy, right?" Cam asked.

"Yes, it was a new chair for his office, and the delivery man had to bring it in and set it up. That gave me my chance. Kurt couldn't exactly lock us all in without it looking suspicious. I excused myself to use the bathroom and then took off. By the time, he realized I was gone I'd made it to the subway and hopped on a train to Queens."

"Then you came here?"

"No. I didn't want Mom to see all the bruises. When he showed up at the first motel I was at I realized he'd put a tracker on me. I still had the phone, not sure why I'd taken it since I couldn't make a call. I changed motels, bought a bunch of burner phones, and waited to heal."

"What a nightmare for you, baby, I'm so sorry I didn't know," Pam said as she kneeled down and hugged her daughter.

"I told you, it's not your fault. I did this to myself. I was one of those too stupid to live women that we all hate."

"No, don't say that."

"It's true. But I won't be making that mistake again," Jen said, the pain and determination evident in her voice.

"When I'd healed enough to pass for normal and called Mom and to tell her I was coming home. But when I saw the news and my picture on television, I had to revise the plan. I was worried the police would find me and drag me back to him, so I colored my hair, exchanged my clothing at the second-hand store and changed my name. And now you know it all."

"Well fuck. That's a hell of a story."

CHAPTER 8

It was done now. She'd shared everything and should have been relieved, but no, it only made her want to run away. But she was so exhausted, mentally and physically, she probably wouldn't be able to make it outside let alone up the stairs to her mom's apartment.

Grabbing the water bottle and taking a long drink helped some though a double shot of whiskey would have been better. Once she'd started explaining her life with Kurt over the last eight months it poured out of her like an open faucet. It wasn't until she finished, and the sound of her voice died off in her ears, that the reality sank in.

A wave of dizziness hit her hard and her teeth

started chattering. She tried to take a drink of water, but she was shaking too hard to drink it. As her eyes met Murph's the room began to spin, and his face blurred. Closing her eyes didn't help, just made it worse.

"Easy, Jen, it's okay. Try to relax." Her mom's voice should have been soothing but Jen's shame and regret overwhelmed her.

"I don't feel well," she murmured as a wave of nausea made her gag. A small trashcan was shoved into her hands as she bent over and heaved. Nothing but a little water came up, but she couldn't stop the gagging. She wasn't sure how long she was bent over the can heaving her guts out before the urge stopped.

Jen took a deep breath after she put the small trashcan on the floor and leaned back in the chair. Nausea passed but the shaking intensified as she was both hot and cold at the same time. Goosebumps raised on her arms and her cheeks burned.

"Here baby, hold this on your forehead. I'm going to get you something to eat," her mom said as she placed a cool cloth on Jen's head.

"No food, Mom. Not yet. Just more water," Jen replied. "Ugh, I'm so cold." Before she finished saying it, something warm was placed over her shoulders. Pulling it around her, the shaking slowed.

A male voice said he'd get her water. Damn, she'd forgotten the SEALs were there. If there was ever a time that she wished the floor would open up and suck her in, this was it.

"It'll be okay, Sky. You've been through so much this is just your body's way of dealing with it."

Recognizing Murph's southern drawl, she realized it was his sweatshirt draped over her. It smelled good, like fresh air and something else. Comforting. But were they all still there? She didn't want to open her eyes to find out.

A water bottle was pushed into her hand. Unable to hide behind her closed eyes any longer, she looked around the office and was relieved only Murph and her mother were there. Opening the bottle she took a short drink, not wanting it to come back up. Wincing as she thought about everything, she didn't know how she'd face the guys when she saw them again. One more thing to be ashamed of. The list kept growing.

"Are you feeling any better?" Murph asked.

She should have been nervous hearing him so close to her, but his soft drawl, so unlike Kurt the fucktard's New York accent, soothed her raw nerves. "A little, thanks. I'm sorry about that."

"No need. You've done nothing to apologize for. Everything that's happened is because of the dirtbag."

"He's right, baby. He should never have put his hands on you. You don't deserve any of this." Her mom's voice was full of anger, but the gentle touch of her hand cooled Jen's hot cheek.

Removing the washcloth from her forehead, Jen met Murph's eyes. "So what happens now? Do I have to turn myself in to the police?"

"Absolutely not. You haven't committed any crimes. What most people don't realize is if you're an adult the police can't force you to return home. All they can legally do is make sure you're not a danger to yourself or others."

"Really?" That was a huge relief. With her photo and the reward splashed everywhere, she figured she'd be arrested.

"He knows it too, which is why he's offering a reward. You said he's a lawyer, right?"

"Yes, he is."

"What else do you know about him?"

"Why?" Jen was genuinely curious.

"I'm going to ask a friend of mine to see what we can dig up on Mr. Kurt Walker."

"But why? What good will it do? If he figures out where I am he'll come for me."

"My friend, his name is Tex, he'll be discreet. I'm sure he'll know everything there is to find out by tomorrow even without anything other than his name and address."

"Murph, you don't need to get involved. I can call my attorney and see what we can do. A restraining order, something," her mom said.

"Restraining orders can't prevent him from coming after her, and she'd have to file in New York. I take it you don't want to go back, right?"

"No way."

"Then until he does something to her here, a restraining order won't work. Do you know anything about his previous relationships?"

"No. Why?"

"You can't be the first woman he's done this to. In fact, I'm counting on it. If we can find at least one other, we'll have leverage. If not there are other options," Murph said.

The anger on his face scared her, it triggered a flashback to the night of the beating. She must have made a sound because his expression softened almost instantly.

"I'm sorry, Sky. I promise I will never hurt you, never lay a hand on you in anger, and neither will the rest of my team. We're going to help you get out of this, one way or another. I know it will take time for you to trust us, but you have my word we'll do everything in our power to keep you and your mom safe."

Trusting a man again was not going to be easy, but at least he understood her feelings. He sounded so sincere but so had Kurt. But she had to admit there was something that was different about Murph.

"Thank you. I can't promise I will be able to trust anytime soon or ever, but I appreciate what you're trying to do."

"No worries, Jen, although I guess we should go back to calling you Sky for now. It will be safer to keep your identity hidden until we see what Tex turns up."

"Okay, I'm fine with that. Mom, are you onboard?"

"Yes, of course. I told you I trusted them. I've known the five of them for a very long time and now their girlfriends too."

Jen finally looked up at her mother's face but all she saw was love shining in her eyes. It didn't make the shame and regret disappear, but it did ease them a bit.

"I think I'm ready to eat now."

"Do you want a burger or something else?" her mom asked.

"The burger. Hopefully, I won't regret it."

"I'll stay with her, Pam. Do what you need to do," Murph said before he turned toward Jen. "Unless you don't want me to? If you're scared to be alone with me I can wait outside."

"No, it's okay. As long as you don't grab me, I'll be okay."

"You got it, no grabbing." His smile lit up his entire face and eased the hard edges. She couldn't help but smile in response.

"I'll be right back. Can I bring you anything, Murph?"

"A beer, if you don't mind?"

"Not at all," her mom said as she disappeared through the door.

"I'm going to sit down behind the desk. I'd like to ask you some more questions. If it upsets you, I'll stop."

That he understood her fear and didn't mock

her for it went a long way toward easing her stress. "Yes, but I've told you everything I can remember. Just so you know, I was never like this. I'm a happy person or was."

"I remember how you were when you worked here for the summers. You've been through a traumatic event. Everyone is affected differently by what you've been through, but if it hadn't changed you, I'd have been worried. You need to cut yourself some slack."

Slack? Cut herself some slack. Yeah, that was way easier said than done. Murph was right, though. If she didn't work on putting this behind her, she'd be stuck in this hole of fear and sadness for the rest of her life. Nodding, she finished the bottle of water as her mom came in with Murph's beer and another water for her.

"Thank you, Mom. I don't know how you're not furious with me."

"How could I be? The blame belongs to that mug jerk in New York for putting his hands on my baby girl. I'm glad you came home where we can keep you safe."

"But what if he comes here? If Murph recognized me, it's only a matter of time before someone else does."

"We'll cross that bridge when we get there, okay? Now let me go get your burger."

"She's right, and we have your back."

"Alright, before my burger gets here, what do you want to know?" Her stomach growled in agreement loud enough that Murph heard it.

He chuckled and her cheeks warmed with embarrassment. Thank God she wasn't interested in dating, because after tonight she'd be afraid to know what he thought of her.

Murph reached into his pocket and pulled out his phone. "I'm going to take some notes then I'll send them to Tex."

"Okay."

"Does Kurt have a middle name?"

Thinking for a moment she tried to remember what was on his business card. It had been a while since she'd seen it. But then she remembered. "He has a middle initial on his business cards. It's the letter T."

"Good. Kurt Walker is a pretty common name. Even though we know the law firm and his address, we want to find out more about his background."

"Does he have any scars, tattoos, any distinguishing marks on his body?"

"Yes, an appendectomy scar." Jen averted her eyes when she realized that he'd know she'd seen Kurt naked. Someone needed to invent something to erase specific memories. If there was a way to remove all trace of him she'd jump all over that.

As she watched, Murph typed into his phone. "Do you know anything about his past? Family, friends?"

"The only friends I met were work associates. No one visited unless we hosted a dinner party. Mostly, we had dinner out with his fellow attorneys or clients."

"No mention of a family at all?"

"Nope. I guess that is kind of weird. Isn't it?"

"You dated for about two months you said before you moved into his loft?"

"Yes, we decided it would be cheaper for me to not renew my lease and move in."

Murph nodded and made more notes.

"Did you tell him about your mom?"

"A little, but he really wasn't interested. I wanted to visit but he wouldn't let me come alone and he kept saying he was too busy."

"So he doesn't know you're from Norfolk?"

"I don't think so, but he could have run a

background check on me at any time. I wouldn't put it past him."

Nodding, he two-finger tapped into his phone. Her stomach growled again as her mom opened the door and came in with her burger. It smelled so good and she prayed her stomach wouldn't rebel.

"Here you go, baby. Eat it slowly so it doesn't come back up."

"I know. I'm thirty-two years old, not twelve," Jen said with a smile to make sure her mom knew she was teasing.

"Don't be a smartass. Murph, Jake wanted you to know they were heading out, but he needs you to call him as soon as you get home."

"Thanks, Pam."

"No, thank you. I feel a lot better knowing that Jen has you watching her back. If you two are okay in here, I'm going to check on the bar."

"Go ahead, Mom. I'm a lot better now and you can tell Tony this is excellent," Jen answered as she swallowed her first bite of the burger. It tasted even better than she remembered or maybe she was just famished.

"Okay. I'll be back shortly," her mom said as she closed the office door behind her.

"Finish your burger, then we can talk some more."

"Thank you. I didn't realize I was so hungry."

"I'm not surprised with all the shit hitting the fan this evening. You were about to eat then weren't you?"

Nodding, since her mouth was full, she finished off the burger a lot faster than she should have. But so far it wasn't bothering her stomach. She rarely threw up, but stress, hunger, and fear did a number on her.

Murph asked a few more questions once she'd eaten. Then he told her a little about his team, each of their names and the women they were dating. She figured it was his way to try to make her comfortable around them.

As she listened to him talk, memories of him returned. He'd been a lot younger then but so had she. The first time she'd seen him in the bar, he'd just finished BUD/S and was celebrating. He'd aged well, and it made her wonder why he wasn't dating anyone. He'd told her all about Meghan, Chrissy, and Miranda, three of the five of them.

Her mom got back about a half-hour later. "Sandie and Tony are going to handle closing tonight. I told them since I had a visitor and you'd had a long day that I wanted you to be able to get some rest."

"Are you sure? I don't want to mess up your schedule."

"Hey, it's my bar I can do what I want. Oh shit." Her mom realized Murph was still there. "You can just forget you heard that."

"Are you kidding? We've had bets going for years about who really owned this place."

"Well, you still don't know. Do you hear me? I like things the way they are and if it gets out that I own the Ready Room…well, let's just say I don't need that headache."

"Yes, ma'am. Well except for the team but I'll swear them to secrecy," Murph said with a glint in his eye.

Jen chuckled. It was funny seeing him give her mom a hard time. And it proved how much they liked each other.

"They better or you'll all be banned, and I'm not kidding," her mom threatened. "It really needs to stay a secret."

"Yes, ma'am. I promise. Your secret is safe with us. I'll see you tomorrow after work. I'm not sure if the whole team will be here but if you need us, here are our numbers. Put them on your phone, both of you." Murph handed her mom a piece of paper he'd gotten from her desk with the SEAL's phone numbers.

"Thanks, Murph. Thank the rest of the team for me too, okay?"

"Me too. Although, I'm mortified that they had to hear all of that."

"Don't be, trust me, we've heard and seen a lot worse. Get some rest."

"You ready to get some rest?" Her mom asked as she grabbed Jen's plate and the empty beer bottle to take to the kitchen.

"Yup, let's go." Jen didn't realize how thoroughly exhausted she was until she stood up from the chair and wobbled. Just thinking about sleeping in her old bed made her sigh with relief. For the first time in months, she'd be able to go to bed and be safe.

CHAPTER 9

Murph's eyes popped open at four-thirty as they did every day since he'd joined the Black Eagle Team. His first thoughts were usually about coffee though, but today they were all about Sky, and he had to fight off the urge to text her. The team agreed to call her by her alias until they knew more, but the name seemed to fit her perfectly. Not everyone got up at zero dark thirty, he reminded himself. He'd have to wait a few hours until normal people got up.

As he got ready for PT, he went over what she'd told them the night before. She'd been through hell but so had many others they'd rescued over the years, so why did he feel differently about her situation? There were too many

108

innocent women and children to count and he'd cared about all of them. But Sky triggered emotions he'd never experienced and the need to protect her was almost overwhelming.

By the time he'd gotten home last evening, he'd forgotten all about his promise to call Jake. But his boss didn't forget anything and called about an hour after he'd gotten back from the Ready Room.

When he saw the caller ID, Murph winced. "Hey boss, sorry I forgot to call."

"I figured. How is Pam's daughter?"

"She's scared the douchebag will show up and drag her back. But she was calmer when I left."

"Good. I called Tex and told him what we knew about Walker. He'll be expecting your call in the morning with whatever other intel you got from Sky."

"Copy that. There wasn't a whole lot. But did get a few things to help make sure we have the right guy."

"What she did was damn ballsy, especially considering her state of mind."

"I agree, but she doesn't see it that way," Murph said.

"It'll take time and some counseling like most cases of PTSD."

"Right. I told them I'd stop over tomorrow after work. With any luck, Tex will have dug up some shit on Walker."

"Is she going to lay low until then?" Jake asked.

"I explained to Pam it would be best if Sky stayed in the apartment, especially after the reward was posted. Fifty grand is a lot of money and there are too many people who might recognize her even with her new look."

"Good. Okay, looks like you got everything covered. See you for PT."

"Will do. Night, boss."

As soon as they'd finished PT and he'd showered, Murph texted Sky. It was still early but he couldn't shake the need to know she was safe.

Murph: *Morning, Sky. This is Murph. Just checking in.*

Sky: *Morning. Mom and I are drinking coffee.*

Relieved she answered right away, he smiled as he took a big gulp from his own coffee.

Murph: *You're staying inside today, right?*

She hadn't been happy last night when they'd discussed it, but Pam had agreed it was for the best. It probably seemed like Sky replaced Walker's jail with a new one that was safer. But until they could figure out what made him tick, it was her safest option.

Sky: Yes. But I don't like it.

Murph: It shouldn't be for too long. We'll come by later.

Sky: We?

Murph: Yeah, the team.

Sky: You don't have to. Mom says hi.

He'd expected something along those lines. But it didn't change anything. Nothing except a mission would keep him from seeing her later. Jake and the rest of the guys wanted to talk to her again.

Murph: *Text or call if anything comes up. See you later.*

Sky: *Bye.*

"Everything okay?" Rafe asked as he poured a cup of coffee.

"Yeah, she's scared and frustrated, not that I blame her. She just wanted to get on with her life."

"She will. Did you talk to Tex yet?" Jake asked as he joined them.

"Nope, that was my next call. I just needed to make sure Sky was okay first."

The look exchanged between Rafe and Jake didn't go unnoticed, but he didn't care. Let them think what they wanted. He was just concerned about her welfare. Nothing more. That's it. But the little voice in his head yelled bullshit as loud as it could.

"Make it quick, you've got about five minutes until the briefing," Jake said, as he and Rafe grabbed coffee for the rest of the team and left him alone.

"Copy that, boss," Murph replied. Quickly reviewing the notes he'd made last night he dialed Tex, computer guru, ex-SEAL, and all-around badass. He'd pulled their asses out of the fire more times than he could remember and if it hadn't been for him, who knows if Cam and Miranda would still be alive. Hopefully, he'd be able to help Sky too.

"Hey, Murph. I've been waiting for your call."

"I don't have long, but I just sent you a text with all the notes I made last night. Jake said he explained the rest."

"Yeah. So what are we looking for?"

"Anything we can find on him. My gut is telling me that Sky isn't the first woman he's treated this way. If we can find even one other ex of his, then maybe it will be enough to prove Sky's story."

"Got it. Is she safe? Do you need me to send a tracker for her phone?"

"She's at her mom's, you've been to the Ready Room, right?"

"Yeah, many times but not for years."

"Sky is Pam's daughter. She's using Sky Russell but her given name is Jennifer Turner. The douchebag is offering a fifty thousand dollar reward to anyone with information about her whereabouts."

"I'll definitely send the tracker. Better to be extra cautious."

"Agreed. Thanks for doing this. I know it's not something we'd usually be involved in."

"If it's helping a woman, you know I'm on board. I'll let you know what I find."

"Thanks, later."

Feeling better knowing Tex was on it, Murph went into the briefing room and put his game face on, making it inside just before the captain started. Nodding, Murph took the seat between Cam and Ryan.

It was just before seven when Jen opened her eyes. Disoriented, it took her a few moments to remember she was at her mom's. She hadn't slept in her old bed in years, but it was the best sleep she'd gotten in forever.

Going over the events of the previous day, she couldn't believe the rat bastard had put a reward out. She'd really hoped that he'd give up on her. Not that she wanted him to terrorize anyone else either. There was no doubt in her mind that he would continue to beat her. Leaving was her only option.

Jen sat up and put her legs on the floor. She wanted to stretch so badly, but the pain in her ribs still brought tears to her eyes. Pulling up her t-shirt, she checked the bruises on her stomach and chest. After almost three weeks, they were finally fading into an ugly green-purple color.

Reaching for the bottle of water on the bedside table, she noticed a photo of her and her dad. Was it there last night? Or had her mom brought it in while she was sleeping? It was from one of their fishing weekend adventures. Sometimes they even brought home a good haul. But her mom always packed tons of food for them to bring so they were never hungry. So many happy memories. Damn, what she wouldn't give for just one more moment with her dad.

Still looking at the photo and reminiscing, she jumped as her door opened. When would that end?

"I'm sorry, I didn't mean to startle you," her mom said gently.

"Don't be. It'll just take time. I don't like it either."

"Ahh, I see you found the photo. It's usually in my room, but I thought it should be in here with you."

"We were so happy then," Jen answered. It would be too easy to let the emotions bubbling up come out, but she'd done enough crying for a lifetime already.

"Yes, we were. I'm sure Dad is still watching over us."

"Me too."

"So...how about some breakfast? Are you hungry? I've already made a big pot of coffee."

"I'm not really hungry."

"Maybe not, but you're going to eat. All you had was that burger yesterday. How about some toast? I have rye bread."

"Aren't you the temptress?"

"Nope, just happy to have my daughter home, no matter the reason."

"I love you, Mom. I know I don't tell you enough," Jen said as she wrapped her arms around her mom's waist. "I drew the lucky ticket when I got you and dad for parents."

"I feel the same. Now go brush your teeth. I love you but damn your morning breath." Her mom chuckled. "I'll be making toast so don't dawdle, young lady."

Jen giggled. Coming home was the best decision she'd made in a while. Hopefully, it wouldn't blow up in her face. She couldn't shake the niggling feeling that if Kurt tracked her down he'd do something to hurt her mother, and she'd never forgive herself.

After spending the last couple of weeks in rundown motels, this was like taking a shower in paradise. Standing under the steaming water helped her feel alive again and free. She didn't realize how long she stayed in the shower until her mom knocked on the door letting her know that her toast was going to be cold.

"I'll be right out. Sorry." Her mom chuckled and Jen hurried. "I forgot how nice a really hot shower was," Jen said by way of apology for taking so long.

"It's okay. I didn't start the toast until I heard you come out of the bathroom," she said with a wink.

"I think you've gotten feistier in your old age."

"Who are you calling old?"

Jen didn't realize how much she'd missed this until now. They'd always gotten along except for the usual teenage rebelliousness. Her mom was her best friend. Why had she let Kurt take it away from her?

They enjoyed breakfast together and then she helped her mom clean up. "Now what?" Jen asked, already feeling fidgety knowing she was going to be cooped up all day.

"Well, we could go downstairs and play some pool before Tony and Sandy come in to open?"

"Really? But what about Murph?"

"What about him? I think we'll be safe as long as there's no one else around. And honestly, I can't imagine Tony telling anyone even if he did find out. He's been hitting on me for years and wouldn't want to piss me off."

"Mom! Seriously? Years? Do you like him?"

"He's a great guy and we've gone to the movies a few times. But I feel like I'm being disloyal to your dad."

"He wouldn't want you to feel that way. How come this is the first I'm hearing about it?"

"I don't have to tell you everything," her mom said blushing with embarrassment as she grabbed the keys for the bar from the hook by the door. "So do you want to, or should we stay up here, be good and tell secrets?"

"Hmmm, we could tell secrets while we play?" Jen batted her eyes at her mom, giving her the big grin that usually got her what she wanted.

"Some things never change," Pam said with a smile. "C'mon before I change my mind."

They hadn't played pool with each other since Jen graduated from college and moved into her own apartment. It was another thing she regretted. Just because she'd grown up didn't mean she had to leave everything she'd loved behind, and that was pretty much what she'd done.

She could have found a small bookstore in

Norfolk or close by, and she could have written her book here too. While she enjoyed New York and some of her time there even before Kurt, it was already starting to lose its shininess. If she hadn't met him she might have come home sooner. But there was no changing the past, only moving forward. It was one of her mom's favorite sayings.

According to her mom, Tony usually came in around ten-thirty to start prep for the lunch crowd and since it was Friday it would definitely be busy. They'd have to clear out before he got there rather than take the chance he'd recognize her if he saw her again. For the hour or so they played, Jen felt like herself again but was reminded soon enough when they had to call it quits and head back up to the apartment.

"Are you sure you're okay with not working? I mean I'm capable of staying upstairs by myself. I promise I won't light the kitchen on fire or anything."

"I haven't seen you in a long time. Your face is plastered all over the TV, so I've got to play the part of the mother who doesn't know where you are. It would be strange if I was working. Besides, who wants to deal with all those questions? If you were really missing, I'd be devastated and a total wreck. Right?"

Jen hadn't thought about that and was glad her mom didn't have to go through that. "You're right. I've been so focused on me I didn't think about the fallout."

"Stop that. If you hadn't been focused you'd probably still be with that asshat."

"Geesh, Mom. Your language," Jen said with a giggle. Her mom really had become a lot feistier and she wondered if it was because of Tony.

They went upstairs and chatted for most of the afternoon. Then they baked some cookies and watched movies until dinner. Not long after that, Jen got a text from Murph.

"Murph says the SEALs are here. They want to know if they can come up."

"Of course. I'll go down and let them in."

"I can do it."

"No, you rest. It's your first day off in forever, I can do it," her mom said with a gentle smile.

"Okay, sorry for trying to help."

"Quit apologizing and let me take care of you," her mom said as she went downstairs to let them in.

Jen was nervous about seeing them again.

She'd spent the most time with Murph. After all she divulged last night, she was kind of mortified. And then throwing up, oh man. Not exactly the best first impression.

The apartment seemed really small when the five large men and Halo followed her mom inside. Sucking it up, she stood and greeted the men and thanked them for their help. It was a huge step for her to shake their hands and she was proud of herself.

They didn't stay long, she figured they'd mostly wanted to make sure she and her mom were okay. They told her that their friend Tex was working on trying to find anything they could use against Kurt the jerk burger. That insult almost made her smile. The more she ridiculed him in her mind, the less power his memory had over her.

"Do I have to stay cooped up inside?" Jen asked when only Murph and her mom remained.

"I'm afraid so. The local papers picked up the story because of your mom. People will be snooping around hoping to find you and cash in."

"I can't believe he won't just leave me alone. Can't he just find someone else?"

"Jennifer Turner, you don't mean that. Take it back."

Shocked at her mom's response she realized she'd basically wished the same treatment on another woman.

"I'm sorry. Shit, I didn't mean it. I'm just so tired of being afraid. First in his presence and now hiding from him worried he'll show up and grab me."

"If he does try to grab you he'd be making a big mistake. He can't force you to go with him and if he tries, it's kidnapping."

"It is?"

"Yes. Oh and Tex sent this for you." Murph handed her a new phone.

"I just changed this burner two days ago. Do I need a new one already?"

"This one is special, and we've already updated it with all of our numbers including Tex's if you can't reach us. It contains a special tracker that he developed. As long as you have it with you, we can find you if something happens."

If something happened repeated in her mind. That's what she was terrified of. "Wow, that was really nice of him. You've gone way out of your way to help and I just don't know how to thank you."

"You don't have to thank us. Just don't give up, Sky," Murph said as he stood up.

He looked like he wanted to say more or reach out to touch her, but he turned and went down the stairs. Her mom followed to make sure they were locked up.

"He likes you," her mom said when she returned.

"Nah, he's just being nice."

"No, it's more than that. I've known him a long time and he is not like this around women."

"He does seem nice, but there's no way I'm ready for a new relationship."

"I didn't say you were, just don't count him out when you are, that's all. So what movie should we watch next?"

Later when Jen went to bed she couldn't get her mom's or Murph's words out of her head. There was something about Murph that drew her to him. The more time she spent around him, the more relaxed she became. She wasn't worried about him touching her like the others. But right now all she could think about was Kurt the turd blossom and how to make sure he couldn't hurt her or anyone else again.

She gripped the new phone in her hand and ran her fingers over the screen. What if she let him find her and try to take her, would the SEALs be able to stop him so they could lock him up?

CHAPTER 10

Two weeks later, Jen had read every book in the apartment, watched every movie, twice, and was about to lose her mind. It was like being kept in a cage. She was cranky, bored, and needed to escape. Even a walk around the block was forbidden for now. Her mother had gone back to work after the first weekend. She needed to be at the bar to work whether or not her daughter was missing. At first, reporters tried to interview her, but she'd refused. Soon, they stopped coming around. Murph and Tex told her that the less information she gave out the better. Until they could find something to nail Kurt it was just too risky.

Murph arranged for the other SEAL's girlfriends to visit. Jen liked the women a lot and it helped ease her cabin fever. Miranda was the quietest of the three. Chrissy and Meghan were lifelong friends and it showed since the two of them played off of each other better than some comedians she'd seen. The stories about their girls' nights were hysterical and they invited her to their next one. It would be wonderful to go, but Jen knew it wouldn't happen until the Kurt situation was taken care of.

Jen was surprised when she found out Miranda was Senator Richard Stanhope's daughter. She'd remembered hearing about her kidnapping, and it turned out Meghan's brother was part of the same missionary group and had been kidnapped too. It's how they'd met the SEALs, and Chrissy worked for the FBI. Their stories were scary and amazing with endings like something out of a romance novel. In a way, it wasn't very different from how she'd met Murph. Except they weren't dating.

The more time she spent around him the more she wanted to. She enjoyed listening to his stories and he told the best jokes. Some evenings he'd come by himself and keep her company while her mom was at work. The best was the night Rafe came with him and was explaining how Murph had more expressions than anyone for having sex. When she didn't believe it, Rafe dared him to say as many as he could in one minute. There's been over fifty and some of them were so bad, she was thankful her mom wasn't there.

"Is that what you do with your free time? Just sit around and come up with expressions for sex?" Jen asked when he was done.

"Not hardly. I've just accumulated them over the years."

"I bet," she answered.

Rafe howled with laughter and almost choked on his beer.

"It took a while, but I remembered you from when I was in college. You were such a horndog. Big bad SEAL with a different girl every night."

"Horndog. Maybe we should change your nickname," Rafe said, still laughing.

"Fuck you. I'm not like that anymore," Murph replied.

"The hell you're not," Rafe objected.

Jen was surprised at the look Murph shot Rafe and wondered what had pissed him off. It didn't bother her. It was pretty common that the guys would come in to blow off steam especially after a deployment. When you grew up around the military it was a different life.

"I'm just giving you a hard time, don't blow a gasket, bro," Rafe said.

But even with Rafe's semi-apology, the light-hearted mood evaporated like smoke, and they left a bit later. That had been a week ago. Since then Murph was the only one who visited.

The four walls were closing in on Jen and if she didn't get out of there she didn't know what she'd do. Even the morning pool games with her mom weren't doing it anymore. She needed fresh air for more than the ten seconds it took to go out one door and into the other.

Murph texted earlier to let her know something came up at work and he was running late. Her roots were growing out and she needed to get more hair color. The drug store was just down the street. Her mom kept the keys with her, so she couldn't take the car, but it was close enough that she could get there and back before anyone realized she was gone. It had been over a month since she'd escaped from the loft. Was Kurt the assclown even still looking for her? The news hadn't mentioned it, but it didn't mean people weren't looking for her.

"Screw it," she yelled in frustration. Grabbing her purse from the bedroom, she shoved her phone in the pocket of her jeans and grabbed the house keys. She'd buy the hair color and come right back.

Stepping outside into the back alley, she took a deep breath of fresh air. Okay, back alley air wasn't so fresh, but that small taste of freedom made her giddy. Locking the door behind her, she walked to the drugstore enjoying every single minute of her stolen freedom. Unless it was busy inside, she should be back in fifteen minutes tops and no one would know.

Her little excursion went well until she was about ten feet from the back entrance to the bar. She was enjoying the fresh air and congratu-lating herself on pulling off her jailbreak when someone yelled her name. Not Sky Russell, but Jennifer Turner. Without thinking she turned toward the person.

Shit. It wasn't anyone she knew, but a tall man in a business suit. When he said her name again, she started running for the bar. She didn't care who else saw her as long as she could get inside. If she threw enough of a fit any of the guys inside would keep him from hurting her if that's what he intended.

Except she didn't get that far. Turning to see how far away he was, she ran straight into Murph. If he hadn't grasped her arms, she would have fallen.

"Can I help you?" he asked the man in the suit at the same time pushing her behind him, keeping a hold of her arm.

"I just want to talk to her."

"Who?"

Jen was surprised at how his drawl thickened now that he was pissed off.

"Jennifer Turner."

"I think you're mistaken. This is my girlfriend Sky." Murph squeezed her arm to reassure her. Murph had this, he wouldn't let anything happen to her.

"She turned when I called her name. You're lying," the man's voice was irritated now.

"I'm sure anyone would turn if they heard someone yell out. You need to go back to where you came from. There's no one by that name here," Murph's voice was sharp enough to cut.

Jen peered around him and saw the man take a step back. Six foot whatever of angry SEAL was not someone you wanted to mess with.

"Maybe I was mistaken. Have a good evening," the man said and backed up a few steps before turning and walking away.

Crisis averted, Jen opened her mouth to thank Murph, when he turned toward her with eyes blazing fire.

"What the hell were you doing? What part of staying inside was hard to understand? What if I hadn't been here to stop him?" Murph ground out with his jaw clenched.

His anger freaked her out and Jen pulled out of his hold and took a few steps back, fear flooding her system with more adrenaline than she could handle.

"I'm sorry, I just couldn't be inside anymore," she stammered trying to hold back the tears that filled her eyes.

At her words, Murph must have realized he scared her. He took a deep breath and the anger dissipated as he breathed out.

"I'm sorry, I shouldn't have yelled at you. But seeing you running down the street with that guy chasing you scared the shit out of me. I don't want you scared of me, but you put yourself in danger."

She was irritated, but more at herself and her reaction than at him. Yeah, he scared her when he got mad, but she'd deserved it. He was right, she should have stayed put.

"I thought it was okay, but I should have known people would still be looking. Thank you for saving me."

"I told you I'd keep you safe and I meant it. Now, how about we get inside before anyone else tries to steal you away?" He forced a smile and she appreciated the effort, but it didn't make it all the way to his eyes.

He put his hand on her lower back. "Let's go in through the alley, we don't need to worry your mother."

"Good point. I've been a bear lately. Being cooped up is driving me crazy. I think she's about ready to toss me out."

"Pam would never do that."

"No, she wouldn't. She's amazing and I don't know what I'd do without her."

When they reached the rear entrance, he

gently took the keys from her hand and opened the door, then locked it behind them. The stairs gave him a good view of her butt in the tight jeans. Did it look okay? A weird thought but it was probably from the stress of the last ten minutes. Did she want him to check out her butt? Oh yeah, she was officially losing it.

Murph's heart nearly stopped when he saw Sky running down the street with a suit-wearing asshat close behind. He jumped out of his truck and raced toward her, grabbing her as she ran into him. It took every ounce of willpower he possessed to not take the guy out. But he also had the moment of clarity. If he did, he'd end up in jail himself.

What he didn't understand is why she was out of the apartment. Not that it mattered now. Her cover was blown, and they would have to figure out their next steps since Tex still couldn't find the whereabouts of any of his exes.

Once inside, she didn't say a word to him, just went to the fridge and got him a beer. It was almost like he'd come home after a long day of work, almost. This wasn't his home and she wasn't his woman. Although trying to convince his teammates of that over the last couple of weeks hadn't been very successful. She brought out feelings he never expected and wasn't even sure he wanted.

He watched her fill a glass with water from the pitcher inside the refrigerator. When she turned toward him she seemed calmer.

"Can we talk about this if I promise not to get mad again?" he asked as gently as possible.

Nodding, she walked over to the sofa and sat down. He sat in the chair instead of next to her, so he could see her face. The last thing he wanted was to destroy all the trust he'd gained.

"I'm sorry," she said, as she looked down at her hands.

"Sky, look at me, please. I need to see your eyes." At first, he didn't think she'd do it, but finally, she met his gaze. He'd expected to see fear but was surprised to see fire burning in the emerald depths. He'd take a pissed off Sky over a scared one any day.

"Why did you go out? Especially by yourself?"

"Why? Because if I didn't get out of here I was going to burn it down. I couldn't take being cooped up anymore. I only went to get more hair color. It was a quick trip and just getting outside for a few minutes felt amazing. I'm sorry if I scared you, hell I scared myself. I knew I was supposed to stay inside, but I'm freaking thirty-two years old. Not a child to be grounded."

Her words didn't surprise him, and he couldn't blame her. He wouldn't have lasted as long as she did, but now they had another issue. She was no longer safe, so they had to come up with a new plan.

"I get it, I really do. I'd feel the same way, but you weren't being punished, it was for your protection."

"I know, believe me. And I feel like a petulant child," she said with a lot less heat to her words. The anger evaporated as she realized things were going to have to change. "I'm not safe here anymore, am I?"

"No, you're not. I'm going to call the guys and Tex. We'll figure something out. It'll be okay."

"You keep saying that, and I want to believe you, but it's getting harder as each day goes by. I'd really hoped he'd stopped looking for me."

"I don't think that's going to happen. He even added to the reward. It was on the news earlier.

Now he's offering seventy-five thousand for confirmed proof of your whereabouts. He is determined to get you back and for that amount of money, people won't care if they're breaking the law to grab you."

Jen nodded and leaned back on the couch. As she stared at the ceiling, he sent a text to Jake. He'd call Tex after they got to the apartment.

"They're on the way over. When they get here, we'll call Tex. I spoke to him earlier and he's been hitting a brick wall. But I can't believe that you're the first woman Walker brutalized. He had his act too well-rehearsed and knew exactly how to manipulate you. That only comes with years of practice."

"And Tex still hasn't found anyone else?"

"No, not a single long-term relationship. He's either very lucky or very smart," Murph remarked as he checked his phone.

"I think it's both. He had a computer at the loft, but he kept his office locked and never let me use it."

"Did you have your own computer?"

"A laptop. Shortly after I moved in it ended up on the floor with the screen shattered. He said he banged into it because I left it on the edge of the table. Then he did a great job of convincing me it was my fault it fell. We looked up repair shops and he took it with him to drop off on his way to work. But I never saw it again. Now I'm sure he just stashed it somewhere or tossed it."

"What a slimeball. Yeah, all of this is too practiced. He's hiding something or lots of somethings."

"That's probably the understatement of the century," Jen said with a sigh.

He hated what this was doing to her, but maybe this was a good thing. Now Walker would know where she'd gone, and they could lure him in.

Jake texted that they were downstairs, and he went to let them in. Sky had gotten out more beer and handed them each one as they came into the apartment. He was relieved she was able to calm down.

They were still talking and plotting when Pam walked in about an hour later.

"You didn't ask permission to have a party, Jen," Pam said as she put the burger on the kitchen counter. "If I'd known you were all up here I'd brought food for everyone."

"It was sort of a spontaneous get-together," Jen replied.

"What happened?" Pam asked, her voice peppered with worry. It must have been hell being a teenager and trying to pull anything over on her.

Jen shrugged. "Go ahead, tell her, Murph."

Pam turned toward her and nailed her with the 'mother' look, one eyebrow raised, and a no-nonsense expression.

"Sky went to the drugstore for more hair dye and on her way back she was spotted. Best guess, he worked for Walker in some capacity, and got lucky."

"Why wouldn't you just ask me to pick it up for you?"

"Because I needed air and space outside of these four walls. I know I screwed up," Jen replied with frustration.

Before Pam could say anything else, Jake interjected, "Actually, it's probably a good thing. Now he knows she's in Virginia. He'll figure we're moving her, which we are, and hopefully come after her himself."

"Moving her where?"

"That's what we're trying to figure out. Someplace secluded but not too far from here," Jake replied. "One of us will always be with her to make sure she's safe, and if he comes for her we'll be there to stop him."

"And if he doesn't? You can't keep this up forever. You're all part of the same team. If one goes, you all go. Who will take care of her then?" Pam asked.

"That's what I said too, Mom. But Tex has a plan to drop enough hints he won't be able to resist coming for me."

"So you're going to be bait?"

Murph winced, it sounded horrible, but it was exactly what they were going to do. It was their best chance to end this once and for all.

"Yes, but it's not as dangerous as it sounds," Murph added. "I will not let him harm a hair on her head, I promise."

"I'm going to hold you to that, Drew Murphy."

Hearing her call him by name instead of his nickname took him by surprise, few people besides his team even knew it.

"I wouldn't expect anything else."

"When is this going to happen?" Pam asked as

she sat next to Jen on the couch and took her hand.

"As soon as we figure out where to take her," Jake replied.

"You could go to your fishing spot, Jen."

"What fishing spot?" Murph asked.

"Jen and her dad used to go on weekend fishing trips. It's not too far from here," Pam answered as she stood up and went over to the desk in the corner of the room. "We still own the cabin. No one has been there in almost twenty years. It might be a pile of rubble by now."

"I didn't think we still had it? Didn't you sell it after Daddy died?" Jen said. "It was a cute little cabin, not enough room for all of us though."

"Pam, do you have the address?" Jake asked.

"Yup, that's what I'm looking for. I have the paperwork in here somewhere," she replied as she searched through the drawers. "Got it."

"We'll check it out tomorrow, make sure it's in good enough shape to use and get supplies. If it's a no-go we'll have plan B," Murph said.

"What is Plan B?" Jen asked.

"You'll stay with one of us until we can come up with another spot."

"No, I can't put any of you in danger. Especially not when you have Miranda, Meghan, and Chrissy living with you," Jen objected.

"Then you can stay with me. I have a two-bedroom apartment. And trust me, I can handle Walker," Murph answered. He expected her to object and was surprised when she didn't. No matter what, Sky was going to have to put her trust in him. Staying alone in the cabin or his apartment would be a big step for her, but there really wasn't any other option.

The team had talked about this earlier. It would work, but the cabin was definitely a better idea. It would be less populated in case something went sideways. And from their experience, something always went sideways.

"I'm not thrilled about any of these options, but at least if we're in the cabin there's less chance of anyone else being hurt," Jen said finally. "Will Mom be okay here? I mean he thinks I'm here right? I don't want him to come after her and use her to lure me in."

"We'll make sure Pam is safe."

"Alright, I guess we have a plan. If the cabin is okay, are we going there tomorrow?"

"Yes, we'll either go to the cabin or my place tomorrow," Murph replied.

"Okay." That's all she said then she got up and went into the kitchen carrying her empty glass of water.

Murph followed her but made sure to stay where she could see him. "Are you going to be okay staying alone with one of us?"

"I have to be, don't I? I didn't give us any other choice."

"There are always other choices. But, these make the most sense. If being alone with a man isn't going to work for you we won't do it."

Jen searched his gaze. It seemed like she could see into his soul. She had to know he'd never hurt her or let anyone else. Just being around her made him happy. Once this mess was over, he wanted to see if they had a future together. It surprised him, but there it was. Something about her pierced him right in the heart.

"Okay."

"Okay?"

"Yeah, okay. I'll stay with you in the cabin or your place. I can handle it."

Promising to love him forever wouldn't make him as happy as this moment. Knowing he'd earned her trust enough to be alone with him was huge after what Walker put her through.

"Thank you for trusting me."

"You'd better not let anything happen to me. My mother will kill you."

"Yes, I will," Pam said from behind him.

When he looked over his shoulder and saw Pam's smile, it was as if she gave him her approval.

CHAPTER 11

After their morning intel meeting, they briefed the captain on the situation with Sky and her mom. He'd had several questions about the veracity of their plan and after going over the details and dialing in Tex, he didn't have any objections.

Murph was approved for a week off and Ryan had the rest of the day to help him do what was needed to make the cabin ready. He'd hoped that the whole team could get the time off, but with the ongoing Iranian issue, it was a no-go. If they were sent out on a mission, he'd have to go, and they would have to come up with another option.

The team would follow their usual training

schedule during the day and at night they'd take turns as extra security at the cabin. They needed to be careful since it was US soil and they weren't allowed to operate at home. Murph wasn't concerned about being alone with Sky but welcomed the extra help from his teammates.

Following the coordinates Pam gave them, there was so much overgrowth it was like trekking through the jungle rather than a park just outside of Norfolk. If the landscape was any indication, the cabin could be a total loss. Depending on how well it had been built in the first place, and after sitting neglected for twenty years, they wouldn't have been surprised to find a pile of rubble.

Lady Luck was on their side. When they finally found it, it was not only standing but looked halfway decent. Murph didn't know what to expect, it could have been a one-room box more like a hunter's blind, but this was a small house.

Using the key Pam gave him, Murph unlocked the door. Filthy, stagnant air made his eyes water, but it wasn't anything a good airing out wouldn't fix. The important thing was that roof hadn't leaked or collapsed, and no animals had taken up residence

They got to work and a few hours later Murph had most of the inside livable for now, while Ryan cut back a lot of the overgrowth outside. He'd have preferred to get new furniture or at least a new mattress for Sky to sleep on, but he'd pick up some blankets and new sheets. If their luck continued and things went according to plan, Sky should be free of the dirtbag soon.

Murph dropped Ryan at the base then went shopping for supplies. Then he swung by his place and packed a bag. All packed, he almost forgot to grab the SAT phone in case reception got wonky. A box of unopened condoms was next to the phone in his drawer. Picking up the phone he stared at the box and actually thought about throwing them into his bag too. But a moment later he came to his senses and shoved the drawer closed. She was coming off one helluva horrible relationship. The last thing she needed was proof that he was as much a horndog as Rafe suggested. What was he thinking? Feeling like an ass, he grabbed his bag and dialed Tex as he ran out the door to pick up Sky.

"Hey, Murph, everything cool?"

"Yeah. Ryan and I took care of the cabin. Ryan did a good job of hiding their locations. It was pretty easy since the place was crazy overgrown. Are you seeing the feed?"

"Yup, crystal clear. It'll record when the motion sensors are triggered on the cameras. If Walker lays a hand on her or even threatens her, we'll have his ass over a barrel."

"I hate that we have to use her as bait."

"I don't like it either. I don't see any other way since I couldn't turn up any other exes. You know that makes me itchy."

"Me too. I don't want to think about what the son-of-a-bitch does when he's finished with them and decides it's time for new prey."

"Me either. I've widened the search for missing person reports of women in Sky's age range. New York might have a serial killer on their hands. Although, this other shit doesn't exactly fit any standard profile."

"I know. Chrissy and Ryan were talking about it and she said the same thing." Murph threw his bag in the backseat and climbed into his truck. "I'll check in after I get back to the cabin with Sky and we can do a system check."

"I'll be here."

"Thanks, for everything."

"What do I tell you guys about thanking me?"

Murph smiled at his phone and didn't bother to answer. It wouldn't have mattered anyway, Tex had already disconnected the call.

Starting the truck and heading toward the bar, Murph should have been searching for holes in their plan and not wondering what it would be like to be alone with Sky. He needed to keep his head in the game, but every time he looked into her deep green eyes he was lost. If he didn't concentrate and Walker showed up, he could put them both in danger. He'd give anything for this to be a cozy trip where they got to learn more about each other and see if there was a future together, but unfortunately it wasn't.

They played a couple of games of pool before the bar opened, and since her secret was out she didn't have to hide from Tony when he came in. After her mom told him who she was, he didn't believe her, and it took him a few minutes of staring at her until he gave her a huge hug. In fairness, he hadn't seen her in probably two or three years. When she'd visited her mom before moving to New York, it was mostly in the mornings before they had to go to work. They'd sit and have coffee and talk about inane stuff that she couldn't even remember now. But she'd enjoyed every minute of it and missed it after moving to New York.

"No wonder your mom was acting so strange. It didn't fit with the friend's daughter staying with her."

"Yeah, well in a way, it was true. Amanda is mom's middle name and Russell was her maiden name. It's how we came up with the name."

"And Sky? Where did that come from?"

"It's my middle name, Jennifer Skylar Turner."

Tony nodded. His big brown eyes were full of understanding. "The last couple of weeks makes a lot more sense now. Pam, you could have told me, trusted me…"

"Shhh. I know, but the SEALs were pretty adamant about keeping it secret from everyone. I'm sorry if I hurt you."

"It's okay, Dollface, I forgive you. But we're going to have a talk later," Tony said with a wink then headed into the kitchen to prep for the day.

"Dollface?" Jen asked, barely able to contain her giggles.

"You be quiet too," her mom answered.

Jen grinned as her mom's cheeks kept getting pinker. "I think there's a lot more to you and Tony than you admitted."

"I'm not going to discuss my love life with you."

"Ahh, see, you said love life. That implies there is more."

Her mom shook her head and banked her shot, knocking three balls in and winning the game. "We're done here now."

"Yes, ma'am," Jen answered following her upstairs with a huge smile on her face. It was times like this that she felt normal again and could forget for a short time how screwed up her life was at the moment. She prayed that the SEALs were right, and this would be over soon.

Murph would arrive shortly and Jen needed to pack. She didn't have a lot of clothes that would be good for camping, all she had with her were the clothes she'd picked up at the second-hand store. She'd planned on buying more, but things went sideways. And there was a snow-ball's chance in hell they'd let her go shopping.

As she filled her backpack, her mom paced back and forth. The closer it got to the time she was leaving the more upset her mom became. She couldn't blame her, hell Jen was worried too, but her fear was for her mother. Every night, her dreams were filled with thoughts of Kurt but last night was one of the worst. He'd been in the Ready Room kitchen with one of Tony's knives against her mom's throat. The bright red drops of blood stood out stark against her light skin. She'd woken up screaming for him to stop, her shrieks had woken her mother and she'd run into Jen's room.

Pam begged Jen to tell her about the dream to help make it go away, like when she had bad dreams as a child. Her parents would tell her each time that if she said her fears out loud then they would go away, but her childhood monsters were far different from the real one who haunted her adult nightmares. Unable to fall back to sleep, she stared at the ceiling for hours. She'd never been more relieved to see the sunrise.

Double-checking she had enough socks and underwear, Jen realized she didn't have any pajamas. It hadn't mattered until then that she'd only worn one of her dad's old Navy t-shirts. But there was no way that's all she was wearing around Murph.

"I don't have anything to sleep in?"

"What have you been wearing?"

"Dad's old t-shirts. I had a few of them still stashed in the dresser, but that's not enough for the cabin."

"Let me see if I have anything that'll work."

Alone, Jen grabbed her current journal from under her mattress. It's not that she didn't want her mom to know, she just didn't want her to know *yet*. It was all too fresh and painful, like an open sore that kept getting irritated. They used to share everything, but she couldn't do this to her. There were thoughts written in the pages Jen didn't even want to read ever again. She wrapped it in another t-shirt and shoved it into the backpack.

"How about these? I know they'll be a little big on you, but what do you think?" her mom asked as she held up a pair of thermals with hearts.

"Where did they come from?" Jen said as she broke into a fit of giggles. Her mother had never worn those. No way.

"Never mind where they came from. Do you

want to take them or not? At least you won't freeze if it gets cold."

"Yeah, and I won't have to worry about Murph putting the moves on me either." She was still laughing as her mom tossed them at her head.

"You could do worse than Drew Murphy. He's grown into a good man. And very easy on the eyes."

"A good man who knows a zillion expressions for having sex. Mom, I'm not ready to get serious with anyone. I won't lie, I could see it in the future maybe. But I am still having nightmares about Kurt the twat muffin."

"I was just mentioning it."

"Yeah, I know." Jen's pocket vibrated and she pulled out her phone to see that Murph was downstairs. Saved by the text. This was not a conversation she wanted to have with her mother. She was worried enough about heading off to the woods with the SEAL. He was so much like her dad, a truly good caring man. But Kurt had broken something inside her she wasn't sure she could fix.

While her mom went downstairs to let Murph in, she grabbed her toothbrush and the rest of her stuff from the bathroom. She didn't have much and she sure wasn't bringing all the too colorful makeup she'd been using as part of her disguise. She hadn't bothered to use the hair color she'd bought yesterday. Ironic really, since she'd gone out to get the hair color and been found. The pink and blue had faded some but whenever she caught a glimpse of herself in the mirror she did a double-take. She was looking forward to getting her usual color back.

Hauling her backpack over her shoulder, she met Murph in the living room. Her mom was right, he was a glorious hunk of man, from the top of his close-cropped brown hair, down to his six-pack, and his muscled thighs she bet felt like rocks. But all that proved is she wasn't totally dead inside.

"Ready to go, Sky?"

"You don't have to keep calling me Sky. Right?"

"I know, but I like it. It fits you."

Jen wasn't sure about that, but okay. "I'm ready. I'm not sure Mom is ready to let me go, though."

"I promise, Pam, we'll be back before you

know it. I will not let anything happen to your daughter. Do you trust me?"

Her mom nodded her head and hugged Murph, then turned and hugged Jen. There were tears in her eyes. "I love you, baby girl. Please be careful and listen to Murph even if you think he's wrong. Promise me."

Her mom knew her so well.

"I promise. I love you, Mom. Try not to worry too much. Maybe you should go to a movie with Tony," Jen said with a wink. It was all she could think of to try to ease her mother's stress. It worked long enough to distract her from their leaving. If she'd totally broken down, Jen would have lost it too.

CHAPTER 12

The sun was low in the sky by the time they arrived at the cabin. Murph wanted to make sure they weren't being followed and took what he called the scenic route. It was just like she remembered, and her eyes got misty. The last time she'd been there was with her dad over eighteen years ago. It didn't feel that long and she could almost hear his voice calling for her.

"Hey, Sky? Are you ignoring me because I called you Sky and not Jen?"

It wasn't her dad, it was Murph. "Sorry, it's been ages since I've been here, and I was reminiscing."

"I was just telling you to stay in the truck until I make sure it's safe inside."

"Didn't you and Ryan put cameras up everywhere?"

"Yeah, but I still want to check it out just in case. So back in the truck and lock the doors until I come back out."

"Yes, Sir." He could be so bossy. But the more time she'd spend with him the more she realized there was a huge difference between bossy and controlling.

Climbing back into the truck, she did as he asked and watched for him to come out. Even with the work they'd done outside, it was still overgrown, and the cabin looked like it had seen better days. She was surprised none of the windows had been broken and the inside wasn't trashed or infested with animals. Murph said it was really dusty when he'd opened it up but otherwise in good shape.

"Dad, were you watching over this in case I needed to come here?" It wasn't the first time she'd wondered if he'd been watching over her, especially lately. There were little signs, like when Kurt had to accept a delivery of the chair that gave her a chance to escape. And now an abandoned cabin for almost twenty years still in usable condition?

Jen jumped when Murph knocked on the window.

"All clear, c'mon. Let's get you settled before it gets dark."

This time he was there to help her out of the truck. He carried in all of the supplies and her pack. Once he got everything inside, she put away all the food and then they made the beds. He'd even bought an extra blanket to throw over the couch since it was so dusty. He was glad the electricity and water had been turned on, but it would be a while for the fridge to be cold.

"Sky?"

"Yeah. Just a minute." She'd been unpacking in her old room. It had a twin-sized bed and there's no way she would make Murph sleep there.

A heartbeat later, he was leaning against the doorframe of her room. "I wanted to tell you I brought a SAT phone. It's in the drawer next to the Fridge. I don't think we'll need it, but we are out in the middle of the woods."

"Right. I'm not sure how good the coverage is. It wasn't something I had to think about when I was here last."

"I put your pack in the other bedroom, why are you in here?"

"There is no way you'd be able to sleep in this bed."

"You wouldn't believe where I can sleep. It's no big deal. Take the bigger room."

"Nope, actually it feels right to be in here."

"If you change your mind…"

"I won't. I'll be out in a minute to start dinner."

"Cam just showed up with a big pot of chili that Miranda made. I guess he drew the short straw for the first watch."

"That was so sweet of her. Oh, is Halo here too?"

"Of course, Cam doesn't go anywhere without him."

Before Murph finished talking, the big German shepherd ran into the room and skidded to a stop in front of her. He was a beautiful dog, who just happened to be a trained soldier. Leaning down she hugged his neck and kissed him on the head.

"Hey, I'm starving are you guys ready to eat or what?" Cam said from behind Murph.

"I'm coming. Are you ever not hungry?"

"No," they answered in unison and laughed, then left her alone to unpack. By the time she was finished, they had the table set and were having a beer. Miranda not only sent chili. She'd made an entire meal for Cam to bring over. Cornbread, salad and even a pie for dessert. She also sent enough paper plates, plasticware, and cups to last them a month.

"I need to call Miranda and thank her for doing this. It's delicious," Jen said after her first spoonful of the spicy dish.

After dinner, they helped Jen clear the table, but she insisted on doing the dishes while Murph and Cam did a perimeter check. Cam left Halo with her and she slipped him some cornbread after the men went outside.

"Don't tell him, I don't want to get in trouble." Then she remembered there were cameras everywhere and Tex was probably watching. Not sure where they were, she looked up and said, "And you too Tex. No tattling."

Murph started a fire in the pit out front and Cam got some folding chairs from his truck. They couldn't talk about work since most of it was top secret, but she convinced him to tell her about how he and Halo became a team.

Sitting outside watching the flames and chatting reminded her of so many trips with her father. She missed him so much and it was kind of melancholy to be at the cabin without him. But being outside and not cooped up in the apartment made her happy. Even though Kurt could show up at any time, for that moment in time it was worth it.

As she listened to the guys chat about sports, she yawned. If she was smart she'd go to bed, but she didn't really want to move. She must have fallen asleep because the next thing she knew, Murph was gently squeezing her hand and calling her name.

"Sky, baby, wake up. Time for bed."

She didn't want to move, the heat from the fire warmed her cheeks, and he's draped his sweatshirt over her to keep the chill off her bare arms. It was too nice to move.

"C'mon, Sky," Murph repeated and shook her a bit.

"Fine, but I wasn't really sleeping," she grumbled.

The men laughed. They knew that was a lie.

Standing up, she gave him back his sweatshirt. "Night, Cam, thanks for being on guard duty. Bye Halo," she slurred, still half asleep. Murph's hand was on her lower back as she climbed the three steps to the door.

"I'll be right back. I'm just going to chat with Cam for a few minutes."

"Okay," she mumbled as she made her way to the bathroom.

Not sure at what point Sky nodded off, he figured it was probably when they were arguing over basketball. If it had been warmer, he wouldn't have disturbed her, but the temperature had dropped, and her skin was cold when he touched her. When he said as much to Cam, he got shit for it, as expected.

"Looks like you'll be wearing that pink tutu after all," Cam teased.

"Nope, not happening."

"Bullshit, the bigger they are the harder they fall. And you, my friend, are toast. You didn't want her to catch a cold? Please, when has Drew Murphy ever been concerned about a woman before?"

"You're so full of shit."

"No, I'm not. You might not want to admit it yet, but it's a done deal. Although it won't be an easy road for her after what she's been through."

"Miranda recovered..." Murph mused without realizing the implication of his words.

"Yes, she did but we took it slow and what she went through was a lot different than what Sky had to deal with," Cam acknowledged.

"I know, and I know it's too soon to expect anything. But I enjoy spending time with her, making her laugh, if that's all it ever amounts to, then that's okay too."

"Tell me again you haven't fallen for this woman," Cam said with a smile.

"Shut the fuck up. And you'd better keep this to yourself."

"Are you kidding? I always find out everything last. I can't wait to spread this news."

"Nothing has happened yet."

"I know, but I see how she looks at you."

Cam was probably blowing smoke up his ass, but what he wouldn't give for even one kiss.

"Whatever. I want to check on her then I'll check in with Tex."

"Halo and I will be on duty tonight. I have

coffee in the truck. You'll know if any shit hits the fan."

Murph looked down at Halo, lying by Cam's feet. If there was trouble, Halo would make enough noise to wake the dead.

"See you in the morning."

"Night," Cam replied.

By the time Murph got inside, Sky was sound asleep. Closing her door most of the way so he wouldn't disturb her, he went into the other room and called Tex.

"Hey, Murph. Looks like it's all quiet."

"Yeah, for now. I guess that answers my question about the video feeds."

Tex chuckled. "When will you guys learn that I'm always about fifteen steps ahead of you."

"Probably never." Murph looked up at one of the cameras and flipped Tex the bird.

"That's weak, man."

"Nah, I just don't want to wake Sky. She's wiped out."

"She's been through all kinds of hell. Speaking of that, I might have found something. Since he's a big deal attorney I figured he had to go to charity events. I've been combing through social media looking for pictures of him and I came across a few of him with a woman from about three years ago."

"Fuck yeah. That's huge, way to bury the lead."

"Not so fast. I'm still trying to identify her. She could be anyone, just someone who was there for the event. Until I can get a name to go with the face, we don't really know anything."

"Got it." He was sure Tex heard his disappointment.

"We'll get him. I'm not giving up."

"I know, I'm just fucking frustrated. I want this to be over for her." He wanted it to be over for both of them. She needed to heal, and he was determined to help her. Because no matter what, she wasn't going to get rid of him. He intended to be part of her life however she'd let him.

"I know you are. I am too. I don't usually have this much trouble. There's something off about the whole thing."

"I've had that feeling since I heard the whole story from Sky. Can you email the photos, I'll see if I can turn up anything while I'm sitting here."

"Sure. I'll send you everything I've got. Who knows if you mention some of it to Sky tomorrow maybe it will trigger her memory about something."

"Good point. Talk to you tomorrow. Night, Tex."

"Night."

Three hours later, he hadn't found jack shit on the woman in the photo with Walker. He was an ass to think he could figure it out when Tex couldn't. But he needed to do something, the frustration was making him antsy. It made him feel even worse for losing his temper with Sky when she'd gone out. Giving up on the search, he checked in with Cam. It was all quiet. Not that he'd expected to hear from Walker yet, it was too soon. Tex left the first set of breadcrumbs for the douchebag earlier, and tomorrow he'd leave the rest. If Plan A worked, he should show up in Norfolk in a day or two. If not they'd fall back to Plan B. Murph prayed that their initial plan would accomplish the mission.

Heading to bed with a book, he must have dozed off when his instant-on button was triggered. It took him all of two seconds to go from asleep to wide awake, and another second to realize what he'd heard.

The shrieks coming from the other bedroom terrified him. Jumping out of bed, he charged into her room expecting to find Walker. Instead, Sky was in bed all alone and screaming.

God only knew what she was dreaming, but it shredded him. Sitting on the edge of her bed, he ran a hand through her hair, trying to calm her. He was afraid to wake her up too quickly and scare her even more.

Seconds later, Cam charged through the front door, gun drawn, Halo at his side. Halo was at the side of the bed sniffing her face when she woke up surrounded by two freaked out SEALs.

The light from the other room shone on her face and accentuated the tears on her cheeks. Murph had to fight his instinct to pull her into his lap and hold her until she calmed down.

"Sky? That was a hell of a dream."

"Shit. I'm sorry. Did I wake you?" Her voice sounded wobbly.

"You scared the shit out of us. We thought Walker was here," Cam said as he slid his weapon into his holster. "I'll leave you to take care of this, Murph. If you need us holler. Come, Halo."

Instantly the dog was at his side. A few seconds later the front door closed.

Murph swallowed back some of the adrenaline racing through his body. "Can I get you anything? Water? Whiskey?"

She sat up, running her hand through her hair. Then she looked at him and even in the dim light, he saw surprise flicker across her face as her gaze strayed down his body.

Shit. He was only wearing his boxers. "Let me go put on more clothes. I'll bring you some water."

"Actually, I think I'd rather have the whiskey."

"You got it. Will you be okay for a few minutes?"

"Yeah," she said as she sniffled.

Murph had plenty of nightmares of his own, been around women and children who had them too. But the blood-curdling sound that came from Sky probably cut ten years off of his life.

After dragging on a pair of sweatpants and a t-shirt he went to grab the bottle of whiskey and two glasses, but she was already sitting on the couch with the bottle in front of her and wrapped in the blanket from her bed.

Not sure how she'd feel about him sitting on

the couch with her, he headed toward the kitchen to grab one of the chairs, but she stopped him.

"You can sit with me."

"Are you sure?"

"Yeah, I am. Besides, the chairs are really uncomfortable."

"That's true." Taking care not to touch her, he sat down and poured them each a shot.

She lifted her glass in a silent toast and then downed it. He had definitely not expected that. Then she held it toward him, and he poured her another one.

"You might want to take it easy on those. It's going to hit you pretty hard if you're not used to drinking."

After she downed the second one, she put her glass on the table and drew her legs up on the blanket. He was aching to comfort her, but he didn't know what to do.

"Feeling any better?"

"Yes. Thanks, I'm feeling much warmer now."

"Whiskey will do that," he said gently. "Can you talk about the dream?"

"I've been having this same one for the last week. Kurt has my mother in the kitchen of the bar with a knife at her neck. Then he slowly slices across her skin and the blood bubbles up and pours out of the wound."

No wonder she screamed like she had. He didn't know how he'd react.

"Now I understand why you needed the whiskey. That's one fucked up nightmare. But that's all it is."

"I know it, but I feel like it's a warning or something. Why am I having the same dream over and over?"

"Stress, fear, you've been through so much in less than a year, it's all piled up and focused on the one person who caused it all. I think your mother is in the dream because you love her the most and she represents safety and home, and he's trying to steal it all away."

"You know, that actually makes sense. Thank you," she said. Some of the color had returned to her face.

"Happy to help, ma'am," Murph replied with a smile.

"You know your accent gets thicker when you're angry or upset?"

"What accent?" He knew what she meant but he was trying to keep the conversation light, help her to relax and maybe go back to sleep.

"Right. Where are you from? Originally, I mean."

He hated talking about his life before the Teams but if it would help her, he'd gladly cut open his chest and bleed for her.

"Arkansas, born and raised."

"Do you ever go back to visit?"

"Nope, haven't been back in years. No reason to." He tried to sound relaxed but whenever he thought about his family he wanted to punch a wall.

His sperm donor had been a mean son-of-a-bitch and a violent drunk. He'd come home from work on payday totally plastered and use his mom as a punching bag. Murph tried to stop him but he wasn't strong enough back then.

"I'm sorry. If you don't want to talk about it, we can talk about something else."

He'd like nothing more, but maybe it needed to be told. "It's not a pretty story. It might give you more nightmares."

When she put her hand over his, it did him in. It was the first time she'd initiated any type of physical contact.

CHAPTER 13

Without thinking about it, Jen laid her hand on top of his and squeezed, offering what comfort she could. The stark pain in his eyes tugged on her heartstrings.

"We can talk about something else. I'm sorry I brought it up."

"No, it's okay. I haven't thought about home in a very long time. It wasn't a happy place. Not even close."

"That really sucks. Even though I lost my father when I was fourteen, my parents were amazing. I forget how lucky I was."

"It's okay. Sky, I want to tell you, maybe I even need to tell you. It will help you understand the man I am, and I want you to like him.

Because I like you a hell of a lot. It sounds lame to say like we're in high school. I know you've been through hell, but I want to be part of your life. To help you heal and to see if there is a future for us as a couple."

Had she heard him right? He wanted a relationship with her? All along she'd figured he was being the hero he was trained to be. Butterflies flew circles in her stomach, and the first blush of hope bloomed in her heart. Maybe once Kurt was taken care of, she'd have a chance for happiness. He liked her. He was right, it sounded like they were in high school, but it was the perfect word. If he'd told her he was falling in love with her, she'd have run as fast as she could in the opposite direction. But like, it sounded kind of great. She could handle like. For now.

"I can't make any promises, but I like you too. You're a bit bossy but you've been so good to me."

He obviously liked her answer, because his smile lit up her world and eased some of the pain in his eyes. "We can go as slow as you like. I promise."

"Thank you. Really. Mom was right, you are a great guy."

"You may not think so if you still want to hear about my family."

"I don't think you could tell me anything to change my mind. But I'll leave it up to you to tell me or not."

He searched her face for something, she wasn't sure what. Then he took a deep breath. For a moment, she was afraid, not that she'd change how she felt about him, but for him, that telling her would hurt him too deeply.

"Rogersville is a tiny town. One of those places you see on TV and they don't seem real. Everyone knew each other and all their secrets. You'd think that if they knew something bad was going on they'd stop it."

"They didn't?" She couldn't even imagine that type of place.

"No, they didn't. My father had a violent temper and when he was drunk, look out. I lost count of how often he'd come home from work, totally wrecked and use my mom as a punching bag."

Jen couldn't hold back her gasp. "People knew he was doing that to her and no one helped?"

"I'm afraid not. The type of small town you see on television doesn't exist as far as I can tell.

There is no rallying around and helping each other. I tried to help her. I'd get between them. But he'd just kick the shit out of me and lock me in my room. I never stopped trying though."

"I'm so sorry." Tears gathered in her eyes just thinking about the little boy he'd been and what he'd gone through. And still, he'd tried to protect his mother. It explained so much.

"Everything changed when I was twelve. When I got home from school there was a sheriff's car with blue lights flashing in front of my house. Somehow I knew they were there for my father and I was relieved. Someone was finally going to do something to help us."

In her heart, Jen knew this story wasn't going to have a happy ending and instinctively she moved closer to Murph to offer him comfort.

"The deputy wouldn't let me in the house. I struggled, I needed to get to my mom. But he didn't let go. Then the front door opened, and they led my father out in handcuffs. He was covered in blood. The bastard actually had a smile on his face. Then they brought my mother out in a body bag. The deputy wouldn't even let me see her."

"So you never got to say goodbye?"

"No, they said it was too brutal for a child to see. I never saw my father again either. He got life in prison and I got shipped off to foster care. As soon as I turned eighteen I joined the Navy."

Tears ran down Jen's face for the little boy he'd been and the man he'd become. His story could have been different if he was less of a man, he could have ended up just like his father. But instead, he'd become a SEAL, a hero, and she'd been lucky enough to have him come into her life.

"Thank you."

"For what?"

"For sharing your story. I am sure you haven't told many people."

"You're right. Only Jake knows about my parents. I guess that's why I've always been afraid of relationships. That I'd turn into my father."

"I don't believe that for one minute." Without thinking, Jen got on her knees and wrapped her arms around his neck, and it surprised both of them. Her heart did a little flip when she realized Murph was holding his breath like she might freak out or something. "Breathe Murph, it's okay."

"Can I hug you too?"

"Yes, but don't squeeze too hard my ribs still hurt like hell."

"This is why I keep telling you how amazing you are, Sky. You left and my mom stayed. You're so much braver than you think you are."

She didn't feel brave, but right now, she could help someone who helped her so many times in the last two weeks she'd lost count. Time slipped away as they sat on the couch, just holding each other. Something changed for her in that moment, like the part of her that was cracked and broken started to mend.

The next few days passed without incident. Murph and Sky were alone all day and then every evening a different one of his teammates would report for guard duty. Tex still hadn't been able to find out who the woman was in the photo. When he showed Sky the picture, she didn't remember ever meeting the woman. She also hadn't been to that charity event.

Someone had to know something. The more time they spent together, the closer they were getting, but there was always that shadow hanging over her head, waiting for him to show up.

The second time she woke up screaming he picked her up and carried her into the master bedroom. He stayed fully dressed and stretched out next to her, letting her decide if she wanted to touch him. When her tears stopped she curled up against him, with her head on his chest. The next night she just came to bed with him.

As he'd promised, he didn't push for more. Having her cuddled against him every night was blessed torture. Even the sight of her in her heart-covered thermals didn't dampen his desire. He'd spend the night staring at the ceiling, reciting the SEALs creed trying to ignore his erection. But he wouldn't have given up a second of it for anything. Cam had been right. He was cow jumped over the moon crazy for her.

As each day passed and nothing happened she relaxed a little more and they fell into a routine. Murph was always the first one up, so he could jack off in the shower. He'd thought he had morning wood in high school, but that was nothing compared to the throbbing dick he had from sleeping next to Sky.

They'd eat breakfast then go for a hike. Then

Murph would check in with his captain and Tex a few times a day. Walker hadn't left the city and Murph's week was running out. He wasn't sure how much more work he could miss.

After talking to the captain earlier he'd found out that he had to report back to work in two days. But with Walker still a threat he didn't know what he was going to do. He couldn't leave Sky without protection.

"Okay, what's wrong?" Jen asked seeing him pacing back and forth in front of the cabin. "Did something happen?"

"Yes, but not what you think." He needed to stop her mind from going to the worst-case scenario. "Walker is still in New York. It's okay," he said as he reached for her hand. Looking down at her fingers intertwined with his, he smiled. They really had come a long way in four days, and he didn't want anything to ruin it.

"Then what is it?"

"I have to report back to work in two days."

"So I go back to my mom's and stay cooped up again?"

"No, we'll have to figure out something else. Or somehow make Walker show his hand."

"He's ignored every trap you set for him, it's like he has inside information."

"Yes, it is. Actually, that's an interesting thought." Murph had a bad feeling that Sky was right and pulled out his phone and called Tex and put him on speaker.

"Did something happen?"

"You're on speaker so Sky can hear you too. And no, nothing except that I have to go back to work in two days."

"I guess we need a new plan, huh?"

"Yeah, and I might have one. We were talking, and she said something that made me think. What if there's something bigger going on here? What if Walker is connected somehow? Getting inside information?"

"It would explain a lot, wouldn't it?

"Sure would."

"Let me flip some rocks and see what crawls out. Later."

"Do you think he'll find anything?"

"I hope so. But even if he doesn't we'll figure it out. I know I keep saying that, but I am not going to let him get his hands on you. He'd have to kill me first."

"I want to believe you. I do. But how long am

I supposed to live in limbo waiting to see if he'll come for me?" Tears gathered in her eyes and it broke his heart.

Opening his arms, she walked into them and he held her close. She was right, she'd been through enough already. He prayed that he was right and Tex would find something.

"I'm so sorry, my sky blue."

Sniffling, she raised her tear-stained face to his. "What did you call me?"

"Sky blue. That first evening when I saw you Ryan thought your hair looked like the popsicle he'd get when he was a kid. It was sky blue pink. That's how I think of you, probably why I keep calling you Sky instead of Jen."

"I don't mind if you call me Sky. I think I'd like to call you Drew instead of Murph. I think it's time." Before he could say a word, she pulled his face down and went up on her tiptoes. After a heartbeat's hesitation, she brushed her lips across his.

He couldn't have held back his groan if his life depended on it. He'd imagined the kiss, her taste, how she'd feel. He wanted to pull her closer and part her lips with this tongue and get his first taste but when she pulled back he released her. She already meant too much to him to risk losing her for a kiss. There would be time for that later.

"Thank you."

"For?

"The kiss. Your kiss." He smiled as her cheeks turned bright pink. No matter how many times he saw it, he'd never get tired of seeing her blush. "You can do that anytime you want."

"Oh yeah? Anytime?"

"Okay, within reason."

That made them both laugh. Murph was about to suggest they take a walk around the lake when his phone rang.

"Captain Knox, sir?" Since he'd spoken to him less than an hour ago, he was surprised to get another call. When Sky heard the captain's name, she gave him a questioning look, but he had no idea what was up.

"Murph, you need to report back to base now. Bring Ms. Turner."

"Yes, sir. Can I ask why?"

"We'll discuss it when you get here."

"Copy that, sir."

Sky started to ask him a question, but he held

up a finger as he waited for his call to Tex to connect.

"I wondered how soon you'd call."

"The captain told me to come in with Sky. Do you know anything?"

"Yeah, you were right. Walker is connected but not the way we thought. He's on the FBI's payroll."

"What the fuck?"

"Exactly. I'm guessing they paid a visit to Captain Knox."

"I agree. I'll give you a call later."

"Looking forward to it."

"What is going on?"

"We're going to Little Creek to talk to the captain and the FBI."

"The FBI? Why are they involved?" As soon as she asked the question, it must have clicked because her eyes opened really wide. "Kurt is an FBI agent?"

"No, but he's probably an informant."

"So they're helping him hurt women? How can they do that?"

"I don't know. They probably have some greater good mission that they think makes it all worthwhile."

"This is never going to end," Jen said as she stormed inside.

"Yes it will," Murph said even though she wasn't there to hear it. He'd see what they had to say but there was no way that scumbag was going to ever touch a hair on her head again.

CHAPTER 14

Following Sky inside, he packed his clothes and then grabbed anything perishable. The rest he'd leave there. Once they got the Walker issue resolved, he hoped he'd be able to bring Sky back for a little getaway. He didn't give a fuck what the FBI said either, the dirtbag needed to be taken care of once and for all. Murph had no doubt that the reason they couldn't find any of his exes was because none of them were alive. He'd probably keep them until he wanted someone new, then he'd kill them and dispose of their bodies.

Thinking about it made his blood run cold. If they were right, Sky could have ended up in a landfill somewhere and no one would have known. He was praying that he'd come down here and try to lay a finger on Sky, all he needed was a good excuse.

Murph loaded up the truck and then went back for Sky. Her bag was packed, and she was just sitting on the edge of the bed.

"Are you okay, Sky?"

Her cheeks were pale, so different from the beautiful blush she had a half-hour ago. Hearing his voice, she looked up at him but there was no life in her eyes. It was like the light went out.

"Listen to me, baby. I don't care who or what he is for the FBI. I don't care if I have to rot in jail for the rest of my life, that man is not going to ever hurt you again. I promised you I'd keep you safe and I swear it on my mother's grave."

One minute she'd been on the bed, the next she'd practically thrown herself into his arms. Holding her tight, he kissed the top of her head. They needed to get back, as much as he hated it.

"We have to go. Okay?"

"Yeah, let's go. I'm sure my mom will be happy to have me back."

"I'm sure she will."

They arrived at JEB Little Creek. He wished with all of his heart that he could have kept her from being involved, but orders were orders, the ones from his captain. Fuck the FBI.

He escorted her into the building and stopped at the front desk to pick up her visitor's pass. Sky had grabbed his hand when he'd helped her out of the truck and she only let go long enough to sign in.

"This is where you work?"

"Yes, it is. We're meeting in the conference room and all the guys will be there too."

"Okay."

When they reached the door to the room, he lifted her hand to his mouth and kissed her fingers. "We've got your back, Sky. Don't forget that."

She lifted her eyes to his. The empty look was gone, replaced with determination. "I won't."

With a deep breath, he pulled open the door and they entered the proverbial lion's den.

When Murph opened the door all discussion inside the room stopped. If that wasn't enough to make someone nervous, Jen didn't know what would. It was like being the new kid in school.

"Ms. Turner, I'm Captain Knox. It's nice to meet you. I think you know almost everyone else here."

The last thing she wanted to do was let go of Murph's hand, but she couldn't exactly blow off his boss. "Captain." She couldn't bring herself to say more than that. Maybe she was acting like a petulant child, but it wasn't at all nice to be there under these circumstances.

"This is Special Agent in Charge Jones. He's going to explain a few things to us."

Beside her, Murph stiffened with the captain's words. She didn't like the whole *explain things* either. It sounded like she was about to get railroaded.

He led her over to the table and pulled out a chair for her, so she was sitting between him and Jake. He gave her a reassuring smile, but until she heard what the FBI agent had to say, she wouldn't be able to relax.

"The room is yours, Agent Jones."

"Special Agent."

"My apologies, the room is yours Special Agent Jones."

Was he serious about his title? Jen was ready to get up and leave already if he was that much of a jerk over his title, what the hell was coming next?

"Isn't there another member of your team?"

"No, everyone is here," Knox said. It seemed that the captain wasn't particularly fond of the special agent either. Knowing how closely guarded they kept Tex, she figured no one was happy that he knew about him.

"Ms. Turner, you had an issue with Mr. Kurt Walker, is that correct?"

An issue? That's what he thought she had. He'd barely started talking and steam was already coming out of her ears. "I think it was a bit more than an issue. He held me against my will and beat me."

"Noted. But you're safe now, correct?"

"I don't know, am I? I'd like to think so, but how can I be sure he won't come after me? He wasn't exactly thrilled when I got away. And don't forget the fifty thousand dollar reward."

"Seventy-five thousand," Jake corrected.

"Oh yeah, how could I have forgotten?" she asked.

"As of two days ago, yes."

"So you see Special Agent Jones," Jen made

sure to enunciate each syllable. "I don't feel very safe."

"We've had him rescind the reward."

"Can you do that?"

"Ma'am, we're the FBI."

Oh and that was supposed to make her feel better? "Why aren't you arresting him? He hurt me and probably many other women."

"All I've been cleared to share is that he's helping us on a case to take down a very bad man."

He was talking to her like she was six years old. Who says 'very bad man' to an adult? If Murph hadn't rested his hand on hers, she might have really lost it. Where all this anger was coming from she wasn't sure, but it was one hundred percent better than being terrified.

"And when you close the case on the HVT will you arrest him then?" Jake asked.

Jen didn't have a clue what he was talking about, but Murph leaned over and whispered into her ear. "High-value target."

"I'm not at liberty to say."

"Meaning you're going to put him in WITSEC. Where he'll be free to hurt other women," Murph was almost shouting by the time he finished.

"Chief Petty Officer Murphy."

"Apologies, Captain."

When Jen looked over at the captain when he called Murph out, he winked at her. At first, she thought she'd imagined it. Did they all hate this FBI asshole?

"What happens to him is no concern. He has agreed to leave Ms. Turner alone."

"And you believe him?" Murph asked more calmly.

"If he doesn't comply he loses his deal. Ms. Turner, I can assure you that you're in no further danger from Mr. Walker."

"Honestly, I don't know how you can assure me of anything, Special Agent. He's a crazy violent man. I don't believe he'll leave me alone until one of us is dead."

"Is that a threat, Ms. Turner?"

"Do I look like I could be a threat? I'm sorry but I've spent the last year of my life terrified, humiliated and brutalized by him. I can't just forget that and walk away."

"I'm afraid you're going to have to. If you

insist on antagonizing him you'll be arrested until the case has been closed."

"Arrested? On what charge?" Cam said.

"Obstruction of justice."

Jen looked at Jake and when he nodded all her bravado evaporated like a balloon deflating. She didn't care what he said, there is no way Kurt would leave her alone.

"From this point forward you are to leave Mr. Walker alone. No more clandestine investigations, no more hacking into his computers. Captain Knox, I expect you will make sure they comply?"

"Hacking? We're SEALs, Special Agent, not hackers. I have to remind you that Ms. Turner isn't under my command."

"I think Ms. Turner understands her situation, am I correct?"

"Oh yes, I understand perfectly."

"Any questions before I leave?"

"Just one," Murph said and waited for the FBI agent to acknowledge him. "If Mr. Walker does come after Ms. Turner, what are her options?"

Special Agent Jones looked surprised at the question. Did he actually think bad guys did as they were told?

"If he does, then she should call me, and I will take care of it. Any other questions? Thank you for your time."

Captain Knox escorted him out of the room.

"Are all FBI agents jerks like that guy?"

"No, most of the ones we've dealt with have been great. This guy must have a hell of a big fish on the line to be this much of an asshole," Rafe answered. "It's been a long time since I've seen someone so full of themselves."

"So what happens now?" Jen asked.

"Nothing. Everyone goes back to their normal lives and we see how it goes," Captain Knox responded as he came back into the room.

"But, Captain…" Murph started to object.

"Officially there is nothing else we can do. Unofficially, Tex will monitor Walker's location. If he leaves New York we'll know about it. For now, that's the best I can do."

Jen knew that was more than she could have asked for. "Thank you, I appreciate that."

"I wish we could do more. But I'm sure you'll be seeing a lot of these men when they're not working."

"She can count on it," Murph responded.

"Does he really believe his own bullshit?" Vibrating with pent-up anger, Murph took a deep breath. Being pissed off wouldn't help and only add to Sky's stress. "We can't just let this go."

"We won't. Just like Murph said. We've got your back, Sky."

"Thank you, for a while there I was thinking they were just going to hang me out to dry."

Murph pulled her into his side, wrapping his arm around her. Realizing what he'd done, he started to pull away, but she stopped him. "We would never do that to you, sweetheart. It's against our DNA."

"Are you done making kissy-faces at her, Murph?" Jake winked at Sky and she smiled. He would have given it right back, but since it made her smile, he'd swallow his retort.

"Yes, boss."

"We have the afternoon off, I cleared it with the captain. Let's meet at Murph's apartment and we'll figure out how to nail this asshole."

"Do you need to drop me off at the bar?" Sky asked.

Murph couldn't tell from her expression if

she wanted to go or not. But Jake took the decision out of her hands.

"Nope, you need to be with us so you can sign off on the plan."

"Okay then."

As he drove to his apartment, he tried to figure out the best way to convince her to stay with him. It was safer for her with him, and after spending the last three nights with her sleeping in his arms, he didn't want to let her go.

"Are you okay?"

"Yeah, of course, well except for pissed off at Special Agent Asshole. Are you okay?"

"Yes, and I'm mad too. But you're a lot quieter than usual."

Not one to pull punches and trying to come up with the perfect way to ask, he just blurted it out. "I want you to stay with me. At least until Walker is handled, but for as long as you want. I was serious at the cabin when I said I wanted to see where this leads. And after spending the last few days with you, I can't imagine not being around you every day."

"Okay."

"Okay, what?"

"I'll stay with you until Kurt is handled, but I

don't know about after that. I'll be honest, I would miss you too if I don't see you. But the main reason is to keep my mother safe."

"How so?"

"If he comes after me, you'll be able to protect me, and I don't have to worry as much about him hurting you. My mother would be easy prey for him."

"Understood. You can sleep in the second bedroom and have your own space. Just like at the cabin, you'll set the rules."

"Thank you, Drew. I don't know what I'd have done if not for you and your teammates. Probably be halfway to Alaska by now."

"You never have to thank me. And I'm very glad you're not on your way to Alaska. It's too damn cold there and I'd just have to come up with an excuse to bring you back."

Feeling a whole lot better as he pulled into his assigned parking spot, Murph helped her out of the truck then grabbed the supplies they'd brought back from the cabin.

Rafe, Ryan, and Cam were already there. Halo ran up to Sky immediately. He didn't know what it was about them, but they had a bond he didn't have with the other women.

"What took you so long? Did you take the scenic route?" Rafe asked as he grabbed a bag from Murph.

"Nah he probably pulled over to try to get some kisses," Cam teased.

When Sky's face turned bright pink, Murph wanted to punch him. "No, we just left after everyone else. You guys need to grow up."

Jake arrived in time to hear what Murph said. "They need to grow up? Aren't you the king of sex talk? I seem to remember a list of them somewhere. I think my favorite is boppin' squiddlies'."

"Mine is 'batter dipping the corn dog'," Ryan said.

"Nah, the best is 'taking the bald-headed gnome for a stroll in the misty forest'," Rafe said with a snort. "Admit it, that's the best one."

Jen looked up at Murph, she'd heard some of them before, but he knew he hadn't said the last one in front of her. It was one of his favorites.

"You actually said that? You do know I'll ever be able to look at a gnome again without thinking about that."

Rafe laughed. "Meghan has the same problem. But I'm pretty sure that is the point."

"It's just stuff I picked up over the years. It doesn't mean anything," Murph replied. Rafe wasn't totally wrong but the real reason was it reminded him that it was just sex, not love, not attachment, just plain old getting off. But now that's he'd met Sky that changed. He didn't want to do the 'four-legged foxtrot' or anything else. No, he hoped that one of these days he'd be able to spend the day making love to her.

"Are you going to go inside?" Ryan asked.

"Yeah, c'mon."

Murph let them into the building and took them up to his apartment on the second floor. Unlocking the door he held it open for Sky. "Home sweet home."

Murph had been in the apartment for about five years and was happy with it until he looked at it through her eyes. Big seventy-inch TV, over-stuffed chairs and a loveseat. The kitchen had a small table for two and the dining room area had a big pool table.

"Your room is down here," he said leading Sky down the hallway, while the guys took care of the other bags. "We can redecorate if you want?" He wasn't used to feeling so awkward, but he'd never wanted a woman as badly as he wanted Sky.

"I like your place. Even the pool table. I'm quite the pool shark."

"We'll have to see about that."

Jake's voice traveled down the hallway. "C'mon you two, I have Tex on the line."

Murph mumbled under his breath about Jake being able to ruin a wet dream, and Sky giggled.

"I heard that."

Sky's eyes opened wide as she looked at him and she shook his head. There was no way he could have heard him only her giggle.

Gathering around Murph's coffee table, they ironed out a plan. It was easier than he expected and technically they were sticking to the rules that Special Agent Dick laid out for them. It wouldn't be their fault if Walker blew a gasket when he saw Sky and hot-tailed his happy ass down there to reclaim her. But if he did, they'd be waiting.

CHAPTER 15

The plan was simple. Jen contacted the local TV station to tell them she'd like to make a statement so everyone would know she was safe. They jumped all over it. Tex said since Walker had originally filed the missing person report in New York, they'd at least report about Jen coming forward if they didn't show the whole press conference.

She'd spent the night in Murph's bed with him like they had at the cabin. Her in the PJs and him in just sweatpants. Waking up snuggled next to him, warm, cozy, and safe started her day with a smile. Then she realized that the press conference was in a few hours.

The butterflies in Jen's stomach threatened to

send her running to the bathroom for the second time in the last hour. When the guys explained what she'd have to do, she didn't think it would be that big of a deal. Except she hadn't realized word would get out and a bunch of reporters would camp out in front of the Ready Room waiting for her and Murph to come out. Thank God for him. If she had to face them alone she'd already be in hiding.

"Ready, Sky?" Murph came through the back door and into her mom's office where she'd been pacing for the last fifteen minutes.

"Do I have a choice?"

"Sweetheart, you always have a choice. But if you want to be free of him and your fear of him coming for you, this is the best way."

Nodding, she walked into his arms. It was fast becoming one of her favorite places to be. He smelled like sunshine and ocean and all the things that reminded her of home. If Jen was honest with herself, she'd have to admit that she was more than a little attached to him. Nowhere near the "L" word, but they were heading in the right direction.

"I can't believe there are so many people out

there," her mom said as she came in from peeking out the windows in the bar.

"You're not helping, Mom."

"Oops, sorry, baby. It'll be okay," her mom said with a gentle smile.

"Exactly, this will be easy. Just remember the endgame and stick to the script," Murph added.

Taking a deep breath and exhaling slowly, she checked her hair and makeup in the mirror. She might as well look as good as possible, even with the sky blue pink hair fading and her roots showing. "All right let's do this," Jen said.

A half-hour later it was done. The news crews were packing up, but most of them had reported live. It wasn't often they had the opportunity for a national news story. Since Kurt had put up the reward it had gone viral. She had no doubt he'd done it on purpose, for seventy-five thousand some people would sell their own mother. It had been sheer luck that she hadn't been spotted until she'd gone to the drugstore.

"So now what happens?" Pam asked. They were hanging out in the kitchen and Tony was making burgers. The bar didn't open for another forty-five minutes.

Murph's phone rang before he had a chance to answer and he stepped out to take the call.

Wondering what was going on, Jen answered her mother. "More waiting. Although Tex thinks the temptation will be too great. We hit on all of his triggers. That's why Murph kept his arm around me. Telling everyone we went on a secret getaway and that I'd already broken up with Kurt was the icing on the cake for a controlling narcissist."

"I hate that once again you're bait," her mom said.

"But they've got her six, Dollface. Do you see the way Murph looks at her? Nothing's going to happen to your baby girl," Tony said as he plated burgers for an early lunch.

Jen wasn't sure she could eat, but when Tony slid the plate in front of her and she inhaled, her stomach growled.

They were almost finished eating by the time Murph returned. "I apologize, I didn't expect it to take so long. The team caught the press conference on TV and said we looked great. Cam said to tell you that Halo was drooling all over the screen when he saw you."

"Seriously?"

"Yup, he even texted me a pic," Murph said as he showed them the photo. "Cam wants to know what you did to his dog."

"I didn't do anything to Halo. I swear."

"I know, so does he, none of us have seen him react like he does to you. It's just surprising."

"Got it. That's who you were talking to the whole time?"

"Tex called after I hung up with Jake to let us know that some of the New York stations had shown it live and others were already teasing it for the evening news."

"And that's good, right?"

"It's exactly what we wanted."

"Now we wait," Jen said almost under her breath.

"Yes, now we wait," Murph answered her around bites of his burger. "Hey, Tony. Do you think you could make five of these to go?"

"Will do."

"Do you want to stay here or go back to the apartment? I have to go to work for a few hours. I don't want to take advantage of the captain's good graces. I think he likes you so that helps."

Jen smiled. "I think I'll hang out here with

Mom. I can meet you back at the apartment later."

"I'll swing by and pick you up on my way home."

She could have argued but what was the point? He would eventually get his own way. She hadn't told him, but she'd come up with a new nickname for him—Mr. Bossy Pants. It wasn't the most original name ever, but it fit him perfectly.

Jen woke up alone, but Murph had kissed her goodbye when he'd left at four-thirty for PT. A piece of paper on the nightstand caught her eye.

I'm sorry I can't be there this morning. Text me when you wake up. You make me so happy.
    Drew

After re-reading the note, she grabbed her phone and sent him a text.

Sky: You make me happy too. Good morning.

Murph: Morning. In a briefing. Text soon.

Sky: Okay

It was strange being alone in his apartment. If she was going to stay, she needed to find a job. She could work at the Ready Room, her mother already asked her. But was never what Jen wanted.

Murph left her the password to his computer, and after brewing a pot of coffee, she started a job search. Two cups of coffee later she hadn't found any prospects, but she wasn't sure what she wanted to do either. Working in the book-store had been wonderful but Kurt had ruined it for her. Giving up for the day, she grabbed a shower. As she dried her hair, she decided it was time to find a salon to help her go back to her natural blonde locks.

She'd left her phone next to the laptop. The blue light was blinking. Damn, if it was Murph he'd probably already be on his way over since she didn't answer. But it wasn't. It was her mom.

Mom: Can you come over to the bar as soon as possible? I need your help.

It was kind of weird for her to text and not call.

Me: On my way.

After ordering an Uber and deciding she needed to get a car or something to get around easier, she texted Murph to let him know she was going to the bar. When he didn't respond she figured he was still in his briefing, and if he didn't get the message she knew that Tex would be able to tell him where she was because of the phone.

Fifteen minutes later, she walked in through the back door.

"Hey, Mom?"

It was quiet. Too quiet. They weren't open yet but even if only her mom was there the TVs would have been on. She checked the office, nothing looked out of place, but her mom wasn't there. Maybe she'd had was in the apartment.

But something didn't feel right to Jen. She wasn't sure what made her do it, but she pulled her phone out of her pocket and dialed Tex as she walked through the doors into the kitchen.

"About time you got here. We've been waiting for you, darling. Now put down the phone and come here. How could you be with that Neanderthal?"

His voice froze her on the spot. It was her nightmare. Except it was real. Like a scene out of a slasher movie. Kurt Walker had a knife to her mother's throat. And Jen knew without a doubt that he wouldn't hesitate to kill her if she didn't do exactly what he told her.

"Okay, I'm putting it down. Just don't hurt my mother," Jen said it as much for Tex's benefit as her own as she placed the phone face down on the metal counter near the kitchen doors. She prayed that Tex had answered his phone and could hear every word. He'd know what to do, who to call, and send them help. All she had to do was keep them alive. Jen wouldn't even consider the option that Tex hadn't answered. That would leave her helpless and her mom most likely dead just like in the dream.

"Come closer, and don't try anything."

"What do you want? Why are you here? The FBI said you promised to leave me alone." Jen met her mom's gaze and prayed she was doing the right thing and wouldn't get her killed. As she slowly approached the man she hated and feared, she thought her heart would beat out of her chest. Fighting the urge to run, she had to be strong for her mother.

"They're idiots. The FBI has no clue what is really going on. I could tie them in red tape for a hundred years and they'd never be able to prosecute me. You should never have gotten away. I wasn't done with you yet." His words confirmed a lot of what Murph thought. As if to prove his point, he pushed the tip of the blade into her mother's flesh and a drop of blood appeared.

"Stop. Please. Don't hurt her. I'll go with you. I'll do whatever you want."

"Of course you'll do what I want. Have you forgotten the rules already?"

Her mind raced and her eyes darted around looking for a weapon to use against him, but he was near the only ones in the kitchen. A shiver of fear slid down her spine like icy fingers.

"I'll never forget the rules, Kurt. But they only work when we're together just the two of us. I should never have run away."

"No, you shouldn't have. Do you think you can put one over on me? How stupid are you?."

Jen's fear intensified as he pricked her mother's neck again. The desolation in her eyes scared Jen more than Kurt. Shaking her head, she silently pleaded with her not to do anything stupid.

"I don't know what you mean," she answered, keeping her voice as subservient as possible. He liked that she needed to calm him down. Had he figured out that her phone was connected?

"You can't placate me with false statements. I'm a lawyer. I've heard it all. But I don't give a fuck if you are lying or not. You're coming with me."

"What about your deal with the FBI?" If he was going to kill her anyway, then at least she could leave them enough evidence that he wouldn't be able to hurt anyone else. But she had to save her mom.

"Don't worry, my dear. They won't know I have you and when I'm done they'll never find your body. I'm smarter than the idiots at the FBI. Did they actually think I was going to help them take down one of the biggest crime syndicates? Stop stalling. I won't ask you again. If you behave I might let your mother live."

"You will never get your hands on my daughter again, you sick son-of-a-bitch. Go ahead and kill me. I'll haunt you for all your days."

"Are you sure you want to push me? I could slice her soft neck before your next breath. Now get the fuck over here."

"No, Mom. Please. Kurt, she doesn't mean it…"

How long had she been standing there? It seemed like hours. Drenched in sweat and shaking, she was almost within reach. She'd hoped that she'd be able to pull her mom away but with the knife against her skin, she didn't see how.

Jen was so focused on Kurt and her mom she didn't realize someone was behind her. Neither had Kurt. One minute he was holding a knife and the next it skidded across the floor as the sound of a gunshot echoed in her ears. Grabbing her mom, she pulled her as far away from Kurt as she could get. Then she turned around expecting to see Murph or the police. The last person she expected to see was Tony.

Jen never saw Tony angry, but there was no missing it now. If she hadn't known him so well, she'd have been terrified by the look on his face, but he never took his eyes off of Kurt and had his gun pointed at his forehead. "Go ahead, asshole. Grab another knife. I'm an excellent shot."

Kurt's blue eyes flashed with fury. He was smart, he'd been caught, and a cornered animal was the most dangerous.

"Jen call nine-one-one."

Hearing the sirens approaching, Jen didn't have to worry about making the call, they could already hear the sirens approaching. Tex had taken care of it.

"I always win," Kurt yelled as he rushed Tony.

Before he got close, he'd pulled the trigger and shot him in the center of his forehead, and he went down like a sack of potatoes. Then he dropped the gun on the counter and hugged them both.

"Are you okay, Dollface? How bad is it?"

"I'm okay," her mom mumbled against his chest, as she clutched the towel I'd used to stem the bleeding, but it had already stopped. We'd been lucky, very lucky.

Before she could ask Tony why he'd been carrying a gun, Murph and the other SEALs charged into the kitchen followed closely by the police.

Murph crushed her in his embrace, then pulled back to check for injuries.

"I'm fine. He didn't touch me. It's Mom that he hurt."

"I lost years off my life thinking he had you," Murph whispered against Jen's head.

"I'm okay, I'm really okay," her mom answered. Tony hadn't let her go yet.

"Nice shooting, Ramirez," Jake said as he stood over Kurt's body.

Murph tried to block her view, but she'd already seen it all. His eyes stared sightlessly at the ceiling while blood oozed from his elbow and head. Still shaking from the adrenaline, Murph's rubbed his hand up and down her back, soothing her. She couldn't fight the urge to get out of there. Away from his body. Away from the blood.

"I need fresh air, please," she begged as her vision swirled before it all went black.

CHAPTER 16

Catching her as she collapsed, Murph carried her outside with Rafe running interference. Jake stayed with Pam and Tony to help how he could, and Ryan and Cam made sure no one got inside the bar. Sure the police were there, but the big SEALs were a lot more imposing.

The last thing any of them wanted was to see Sky's photo plastered all over social media. Privacy became virtually non-existent once the internet and smartphones were easily acquired by anyone who wanted one, and it wasn't just at home. It made keeping the low profile they needed a lot more difficult.

"Rafe, can you get the keys to the apartment

from Pam?" Murph asked. It was the only place he could think to take her that wasn't back inside.

"Yeah, maybe we can get them all upstairs. The police can interview them up there away from the body."

Jen stirred in his arms and her eyes popped open.

"Easy, sweetheart. You're okay, I've got you," Murph said gently. Lowering her to the ground he kept his arm around her to make sure she wouldn't fall. "Are you feeling any better?"

"Yeah. I don't know what happened. Everything was spinning."

"There's an ambulance out front, do you want to go and get checked out?"

"No way. If anyone needs to be checked it's Mom," Jen said. "Where is she? Is she okay?"

"She's fine. Rafe went to get the keys for the apartment and so we can get you all upstairs. The crime scene team will be in there for a while and I'd rather you be away from the body."

She shuddered in his arms obviously replaying her memories. "I didn't know Tony had a gun or even knew how to shoot one."

"And a license for concealed carry too. I over-heard him telling the police," Rafe said as he returned with her mom and the keys.

"Where is he?" Jen asked.

"The police are talking to him. Jake is going to stay with him, and we have Tex on standby," Rafe said as he unlocked the door to the apartment to get them upstairs.

"Does that mean he heard everything Kurt said?"

"Yup, he heard and recorded all of it. If the police try to charge Tony, we should have plenty of information to make sure they can't. Tex also sent the police to Walker's apartment in New York, based on what he said about the women. They found a box of 'trophies' from his kills hidden in his office. He'd been doing it for a long time. And it's over now because of your bravery," Murph said. "This could have gone very wrong if you hadn't called Tex."

Inside the apartment, Rafe helped Pam to her room so she could lie down. Murph now knew where Sky got her inner strength. Pam impressed the hell out of him. She hadn't panicked even with the knife against her throat.

"I'm so grateful he was there to answer the call," Jen said as she sat on the couch.

"Me too, sweetheart. I just found you and I'm not letting you go. I don't want to think about a life without you in it." Pulling her close to his side, he tilted her head up so he could see her eyes. "I'm going to kiss you now. Really kiss you. If it's too soon or too much, tell me now."

Instead of answering she reached up and pulled his face to hers. Her lips were cool against his and so soft. He wanted to let her set the pace the fear of almost losing her was too much. His tongue slid between her lips and he swept her mouth, learning her taste.

Her arms slid around his neck as he lifted her onto his lap. He needed more and only his iron willpower stopped him from carrying her into her room. His willpower and the police investigators who'd just come into the apartment.

When the news broke that Kurt Walker, the famous New York attorney was a serial killer and that Jen was the only survivor, they were inundated with requests for interviews. It was like a circus. But she just wanted to hide from it all. The less she said his name the better as far as she was concerned. Just thinking about him gave her a panic attack, even knowing he was dead.

Two weeks later, Murph and his team had left on a mission. Jen was a wreck, and she realized how much she'd relied on her SEAL. Every noise freaked her out, and she had nightmares every night. Her only distraction was helping get the bar ready for the reopening celebration.

She'd been alone for three days when Chrissy called to invite her over for a girls' night. They were remarkable women and when she told them, so they tried to convince her she was too.

"You're just a remarkable, maybe more so. You saved yourself, and not just once, you had to do it twice," Miranda reminded her.

"Exactly, you're a hero, you saved your mom too. Rafe said Tex keeps talking about how you had the forethought to call him," Meghan told her.

"I didn't really. It was just luck. I called him because I couldn't shake the feeling that something was wrong. Then I went through the doors into the kitchen and saw him. I'd already dialed the number, but when he saw the phone in my hand he didn't know it. I just prayed that Tex would pick up."

"Okay, but you still did it and kept the fucker from even realizing it was an open line," Chrissy added.

When Jen heard Chrissy's story she couldn't believe how the woman had taken out a terrorist and saved Ryan. That was hero material, not her. When she went into the kitchen to get some water, Miranda followed her in.

"Are you okay?"

"Yeah, mostly. If I could get rid of the nightmares that would help."

"Have you thought about talking to someone?"

"Murph mentioned it, but I don't know. I'd have to rehash all of it and I'm already a wreck."

"Here." Miranda handed her a business card. "I've been seeing her since the kidnapping. She's really amazing. I think she'd be able to help you."

"I don't know," Jen really didn't want to tell another stranger what an ass she'd been.

"Just take the card. Then if you change your mind, you have her number."

A few days later Miranda called to check on her. After they spoke some more, Jen broke down and called to make an appointment. Even after only one week, it made a huge difference, mostly because she learned that she didn't have to hide her feelings or her fear. That it was all okay. It would be a long process until she stopped jumping at shadows, but now she knew she'd get there, and she couldn't wait for Murph to get home to tell him.

When Murph had walked in the day before, she nearly jumped for joy. He'd been gone two and a half weeks, but she'd survived with the help of her friends and new therapist. Even though she'd been doing so much better, sleeping curled up against Murph made her heart happier than she could ever remember.

They hadn't done more than kissing. Murph was waiting for her to be ready, but she was worried she'd freak out in the middle and ruin their relationship. She'd shared her worries in counseling and Dr. Marsh told her when she was ready she'd know. Jen wasn't yet, but she wanted to take things a little further. Now that Murph was home she had a plan.

After almost two months of hard work and lots of changes, it was finally time to reopen the Ready Room. When they opened the doors, she and her mom were surprised how many people were waiting to get in. Apparently, they were famous now that their chef had taken out a New York serial killer. Tony didn't want the notoriety. Her mom was so proud of him that she had a plaque made and hung it behind the bar. They'd also finally started officially dating. Jen couldn't have been happier for her. She'd been alone for too long and deserved to find love again.

Her mom suggested she put a reserved sign on the team's usual table. It had been a good idea because by the time they arrived there wouldn't have been room for all of them and the women.

Murph came to find her since she'd gone early to help finish setting up for the celebration. Her back was to the door when he came in and swept her up in his arms and twirled her around then put her back down. It's when she realized she really was healing. In the past, she'd have been totally freaked out, full-on panic attack.

Being in his arms gave her butterflies but they were the good ones.

"Hi, sweetheart."

"Hi. Do you realize you picked me up from behind, right?"

"I was so excited to see you I didn't even think. Are you okay?"

"Yes, I'm very okay. For the first time in ages."

"Really?"

"Yes, Miranda was right, Dr. Marsh is amazing."

"I can't tell you how happy that makes me. Seeing you smile without the shadows in your eyes is the best gift ever."

"Oh yeah? Maybe I can top that later," she said with a wink, knowing her cheeks had to be bright pink from how hot they were.

"I like the sound of that. Are you going to be working all night?"

"No, she's not. She's done. You've done enough, Jen. Go have fun with your man."

"Thanks, Mom. If you need me let me know."

"I won't. Take good care of her, Murph."

"I intend too. I need to take care of something, how about you go on out and I'll meet you at the table?"

"Are you sure? I can wait, I don't mind."

"Nah, I'll be right there."

Wondering what he was up to, she went out and joined their friends. Halo came over as soon as she sat down and waited for his hug and kiss. They had a connection she couldn't understand, and it made her giggle that it kind of made Cam jealous.

"Oh my God. He did it," Rafe said.

"Who did what?" she asked as she looked up from hugging Halo.

Murph was heading across the bar to catcalls and whistles while balancing a loaded tray with beer and mugs. She didn't understand why they were laughing until he got closer.

"I guess he admits defeat," Jake said with a chuckle.

The only bet she knew about was the one Meghan and Chrissy had told her about It was over a year ago. The guys bet him if he fell for a woman, he'd have to serve them beer in a pink tutu.

Then he got closer and the crowd parted as he approached the table wearing a bright pink tutu. Knowing what it meant, her heart melted.

The worst year of her life was behind her, and there was nothing but blue skies ahead.

Jake couldn't have been happier for Murph and Sky. They'd both been through hell to find their happiness. It made him wonder if he'd ever be able to convince Dawn to change her mind and move east. As he glanced over at Rafe, he wondered what he'd say if he knew that Jake was dating his sister and had been for over a year. He'd probably want to take his head off.

Stubbornness must run thick in the Buchanan family, but he didn't give up easily. She didn't want to get involved with another military guy because of the kids. But he loved them, and he was getting up in years for being an operator. When they talked about it she told him if he did he'd end up resenting her. Yeah, she was stubborn, but also beautiful, smart, and had stolen his heart.

The celebration was in full swing and when his phone vibrated in his pocket. Seeing it was Dawn, he stepped outside since it was too damn loud to hear anything.

"Hey babe, what's up?"

"Jake, I don't know what to do. Chase is missing. He didn't come home after school."

Fuck. Chase was only eleven, where the hell could he have gone?

"Did you call his friends?"

"Yes, he's not anywhere. No one has seen him."

"Did you call the police?"

"Yes, they are on their way over. I can't lose him too, Jake. I just can't."

He could barely understand her. She was crying so hard. "Hold on, Dawn. I'll get a flight and be there as soon as I can."

The End

I hope you enjoyed SEAL's Sky. Look for Dawn and Jake's story,, SEAL's Angel, releasing in July 2020.

. . .

Authors Note: This book while fictional deals with the very real subject of abuse. If you or someone you know needs help there are options out there. Please reach out to friends, family, or one of the many organizations. You are not alone

National Domestic Abuse Hotline: 1-800-799-7233

ABOUT THE AUTHOR

Lynne St. James has been writing for as long as she can remember. She has series in romantic suspense, contemporary, new adult and paranormal. She lives in the mostly sunny state of Florida with her husband, Yorkie-poo and an orange tabby named Pumpkin who thinks he rules them all.

When Lynne's not writing about second chances and conquering adversity with happily ever afters, she's drinking coffee and reading or crocheting.

Where to find Lynne:

Email: lynne@lynnestjames.com
Amazon: https://amzn.to/2sgdUTe
BookBub: https://www.bookbub.com/authors/lynne-st-james
Facebook: https://www.facebook.com/authorLynneStJames

Website: http://lynnestjames.com

Instagram: https://www.instagram.com/lynnestjames/

Pinterest: https://www.pinterest.com/lynnestjames5

VIP Newsletter sign-up: http://eepurl.com/bT99Fj

Taming Chaos

Seducing Wrath

Music under the Mistletoe – A Raining Chaos Christmas (Novella)

Tempting Flame

Anamchara

Embracing Her Desires

Embracing Her Surrender

Embracing Her Love

The Vampires of Eternity

Twice Bitten Not Shy

Twice Bitten to Paradise

Twice Bitten and Bewitched

Want to be one of the first to learn about Lynne St. James's new releases? Sign up for her newsletter filled with exclusive VIP news and contests! http://eepurl.com/bT99Fj

There are many more books in this fan fiction world than listed here, for an up-to-date list go to www.AcesPress.com

You can also visit our Amazon page at: http://www.amazon.com/author/operationalpha

Special Forces: Operation Alpha World

Christie Adams: Charity's Heart

Denise Agnew: Dangerous to Hold

Shauna Allen: Awakening Aubrey

Brynne Asher: Blackburn

Linzi Baxter: Unlocking Dreams

Jennifer Becker: Hiding Catherine

Alice Bello: Shadowing Milly

Heather Blair: Rescue Me

Anna Blakely: Rescuing Gracelynn

Amy Briggs: Saving Sarah

Julia Bright: Saving Lorelei

Victoria Bright: Surviving Savage

Cara Carnes: Protecting Mari

Kendra Mei Chailyn: Beast

Melissa Kay Clarke: Rescuing Annabeth

Samantha A. Cole: Handling Haven

Sue Coletta: Hacked

Melissa Combs: Gallant

Anne Conley: Redemption for Misty

KaLyn Cooper: Rescuing Melina

Liz Crowe: Marking Mariah

Sarah Curtis: Securing the Odds

Jordan Dane: Redemption for Avery

Tarina Deaton: Found in the Lost

Aspen Drake, Intense

KL Donn: Unraveling Love

Riley Edwards: Protecting Olivia

PJ Fiala: Defending Sophie

Nicole Flockton: Protecting Maria

Michele Gwynn: Rescuing Emma

Casey Hagen: Shielding Nebraska

Desiree Holt: Protecting Maddie

Kathy Ivan: Saving Sarah

Kris Jacen, Be With Me

Jesse Jacobson: Protecting Honor

Silver James: Rescue Moon

Becca Jameson: Saving Sofia

Kate Kinsley: Protecting Ava

Heather Long: Securing Arizona

Gennita Low: No Protection

Kirsten Lynn: Joining Forces for Jesse

Margaret Madigan: Bang for the Buck

Kimberly McGath: The Predecessor

Rachel McNeely: The SEAL's Surprise Baby
KD Michaels: Saving Laura
Lynn Michaels, Rescuing Kyle
Wren Michaels: The Fox & The Hound
Kat Mizera: Protecting Bobbi
Keira Montclair, Wolf and the Wild Scots
Mary B Moore: Force Protection
LeTeisha Newton: Protecting Butterfly
Angela Nicole: Protecting the Donna
MJ Nightingale: Protecting Beauty
Sarah O'Rourke: Saving Liberty
Victoria Paige: Reclaiming Izabel
Anne L. Parks: Mason
Debra Parmley: Protecting Pippa
Lainey Reese: Protecting New York
TL Reeve and Michele Ryan: Extracting Mateo
Elena M. Reyes: Keeping Ava
Angela Rush: Charlotte
Rose Smith: Saving Satin
Jenika Snow: Protecting Lily
Lynne St. James: SEAL's Spitfire
Dee Stewart: Conner
Harley Stone: Rescuing Mercy
Jen Talty: Burning Desire
Reina Torres, Rescuing Hi'ilani
Megan Vernon: Protecting Us

Police and Fire: Operation Alpha World

Freya Barker: Burning for Autumn

Julia Bright, Justice for Amber

KaLyn Cooper: Justice for Gwen

Aspen Drake: Sheltering Emma

Deanndra Hall: Shelter for Sharla

Barb Han: Kace

EM Hayes: Gambling for Ashleigh

CM Steele: Guarding Hope

Reina Torres: Justice for Sloane

Stacey Wilk: Stage Fright

Tarpley VFD Series

Silver James, Fighting for Elena

Deanndra Hall, Fighting for Carly

Haven Rose, Fighting for Calliope

MJ Nightingale, Fighting for Jemma

TL Reeve, Fighting for Brittney

Nicole Flockton, Fighting for Nadia

As you know, this book included at least one character from Susan Stoker's books. To check out more, see below.

SEAL of Protection: Legacy Series
Securing Caite
Securing Brenae (novella)
Securing Sidney
Securing Piper
Securing Zoey
Securing Avery (May 2020)
Securing Kalee (Sept 2020)

Delta Team Two Series
Shielding Gillian (Apr 2020)
Shielding Kinley (Aug 2020)
Shielding Aspen (Oct 2020)
Shielding Riley (Jan 2021)
Shielding Devyn (TBA)
Shielding Ember (TBA)
Shielding Sierra (TBA)

Delta Force Heroes Series
Rescuing Rayne (FREE!)

Rescuing Aimee (novella)

Rescuing Emily

Rescuing Harley

Marrying Emily (novella)

Rescuing Kassie

Rescuing Bryn

Rescuing Casey

Rescuing Sadie (novella)

Rescuing Wendy

Rescuing Mary

Rescuing Macie (Novella)

Badge of Honor: Texas Heroes Series

Justice for Mackenzie (FREE!)

Justice for Mickie

Justice for Corrie

Justice for Laine (novella)

Shelter for Elizabeth

Justice for Boone

Shelter for Adeline

Shelter for Sophie

Justice for Erin

Justice for Milena

Shelter for Blythe

Justice for Hope

Shelter for Quinn
Shelter for Koren
Shelter for Penelope

SEAL of Protection Series

Protecting Caroline (FREE!)
Protecting Alabama
Protecting Fiona
Marrying Caroline (novella)
Protecting Summer
Protecting Cheyenne
Protecting Jessyka
Protecting Julie (novella)
Protecting Melody
Protecting the Future
Protecting Kiera (novella)
Protecting Alabama's Kids (novella)
Protecting Dakota

New York Times, USA Today and *Wall Street Journal*
Bestselling Author Susan Stoker has a heart as
big as the state of Tennessee where she lives, but
this all American girl has also spent the last
fourteen years living in Missouri, California,
Colorado, Indiana, and Texas. She's married to a

retired Army man who now gets to follow *her* around the country.

www.stokeraces.com
www.AcesPress.com
susan@stokeraces.com

Made in the USA
Monee, IL
14 April 2022

93862697R00144